LAURA ELLEN

RAINBOW GREY

EYE OF THE STORM

Farshore

RAY GREY

The first Rainbow Weatherling in over a thousand years!

Has LOTS of extra magical abilities called rainbow gifts.

NiM

Cloud-cat!

LOVES to eat contrail cobbler (and any other leftovers)!

Often explodes and reforms with his limbs missing.

SNOWDEN EVERFREEZE

Snow Weatherling.

His ears erupt with snowflakes when he's thinking.

Has a school attendance record of one hundred and two percent.

DROPLETT DEWBELLS

Rain Weatherling.

Wants to be a puddle-porting champion when she grows up.

Is the Weather Wobbler Sky Academy Team Captain!

NEPHIA WEATHERWART

Cloud Weatherling.

The best detective in the Weatherlands.

Has a cloud-slug called Mr Steve.

LA BLAZE DELIGHT

Sun Weatherling.

Almost went Rogue but decided to turn over a new leaf.

Helps Ray to learn her rainbow weather magic.

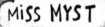

MISS MYST

Rain Weatherling.

The deputy head teacher at Sky Academy.

Hardly ever smiles.

AUNT FOGGALEENA

Cloud Weatherling.

Loves hosting puff pod parties.

Is suspicious of rainbow weather magic.

CLOUDIMULUS SUBURBS

SUNKEEPER CONSERVATORY

FLURRY MOUNTAINS

SUNFLOWER FIELD

BROLLY LANE

DRIPPING-DOWN VILLAGE

CRACKLING CAVES

VALLEY OF WINDS

CHAPTER 1

THE VON FLUFF PUFF POD PARTY

It was a sunny Sunday afternoon in the Forest of Fahrenheits, the perfect place for a puff pod party.

Ten-year-old Ray Grey and her best friend Snowden Everfreeze were perched on a tree stump next to the puff pod patch, recovering from a game of Musical Clouds. Ray had *almost* won, but her cloud-cat, Nim, had exploded, sending Ray plummeting to the ground with a BOMP.

'This is the ninth puff pod party I've been to and I've *still* never won a game of Musical Clouds,' Ray groaned, pushing her long rainbow-coloured hair out of her face. The game had made it even messier than usual. 'Maybe next time, eh?' She tickled Nim under the chin. He purred joyfully and morphed into a heart shape.

'*TEN MINUTES UNTIL THE PUFF POD PICKING*!' screeched Ray's Aunt Foggaleena, making the friends jump. A cloud-sparrow on her shoulder made an ear-piercing chirp. 'Just ten minutes until my DARLING Cloudiculus receives his cloud-creature for life!'

A flurry of snowflakes erupted from Snowden's left ear. This always happened when he was thinking. Ray called them *think-flakes*. Snowden was one of the kindest, cleverest Snow Weatherlings ever and one of Ray's best friends.

'I wonder what your baby cousin's

cloud-creature will be?' he asked, unwrapping
a neatly assembled drizzle-pickle sandwich.

'Cloudiculus will pick some sort of cloud-
bird, I expect,' said Ray, as she munched on a
lightning scone. 'Every Von Fluff cousin has
picked a cloud-bird.' Ray nodded towards Aunt
Foggaleena's other eight children. They all had
cloud-birds perched on their shoulders, tweeting
or squawking or chirping.

The youngest of Ray's cousins, Cloudiculus
Von Fluff, was turning one that day, and it was
tradition for a Cloud Weatherling to pick a puff
pod on their first birthday. Once picked, a tiny
cloud-creature would emerge and bond with the
young Cloud Weatherling. Together they would
learn to create beautiful cloud magic and be
together forever.

The puff pod parties were always a jolly affair
with lots of aunts and uncles gathering to catch up
on family gossip. But, for Ray, this year's puff pod
party was special. This was the first time she had
seen her extended family since her life had been

turned upside down six months ago.

'I bet your aunts and uncles are really excited to hear all about your new magic!' said Snowden with a grin.

'Hmmm. MOST of them,' said Ray. 'Uncle Billow and Aunt Teensy were so happy they couldn't stop raining. But Aunt Foggaleena . . . Let's just say she likes me even LESS now.'

Snowden let out a long whistle. 'That doesn't seem very fair.'

'It's OK,' Ray replied with a smile, her one blue eye and one purple eye both sparkling. 'Because I'll show her that I can be a mighty Rainbow Weatherling, protecting the Earth and skies. And I'll be an AWESOME Earth Explorer too!'

She fist-pumped the air, sending a stream of colours surging through the treetops. Ray grimaced. 'I just need to learn to CONTROL my magic first,' she added, frowning at her fist.

While all Weatherlings had one form of weather magic – snow, wind, rain, sun, cloud or thunder 'n' lightning – Ray was born with no magic at all. In fact, nobody on her mother's side of the family had *ever* had any weather magic. But during a forbidden trip to Earth, Ray had found a black crystal and unleashed an ancient power the world hadn't seen for over a thousand years . . . *rainbow weather magic*! It turned out that Ray was a Rainbow Weatherling, which meant that she could control all the other weather magic. Or at least she would be able to, when she learned how to use her magic properly.

Aunt Foggaleena marched over to Ray and looked her up and down disapprovingly. 'When it's time for Cloudiculus to pick a puff pod, *you* stay over here,' she hissed. 'I want everything to go *perfectly* and I can't risk ANY *strange* magic that might cause a problem.'

'You don't have to worry about a thing, Aunty.

I won't do anything "strange",' said Ray, wiggling her fingers around and pulling a funny face.

Aunt Foggaleena glared. 'Hmm. Keep that explosive feline of yours away too.' She turned on her heel and strutted back into the crowd with her cloud-sparrow following close behind.

Snowden shook his head. 'Your aunt sure has a breeze in her bonnet!'

'Told you,' said Ray. 'Since the whole rainbow thing, she doesn't trust me at all, and she's NEVER liked poor Nim.'

The cloud-cat wrapped himself around Ray's shoulders and purred. Nim had been born with a rare glitch that made him explode a lot, so it was impossible for him to bond with a Cloud Weatherling or be a real cloud like the ones humans saw in the sky. Ray had found Nim abandoned as a cloud-kitten, and since then, they'd never been apart. They might not have been bonded by magic, but their bond of love was unbreakable.

One of Ray's little cousins skipped over

happily with her cloud-owl nestled in her arms.
A young Wind Weatherling followed close
behind, looking a little nervous.

'Hello, Drift,' said Ray with a wave.

'Raaaaay, can you show my friend Flow your
rainbows?' Drift asked. Her cloud-owl hooted as
if repeating the question.

Ray shook her head. 'Sorry, Drift, I don't
think your mum would be too happy if I used my
magic here.'

'Pleeeeeeeeease!' urged Drift. 'My friend
Flow finks your magic is scary, but I told
her it's not!'

Ray frowned. 'Scary?'

Flow looked up shyly.
'I heard that your magic
wasn't like ours,' she
whispered.

Ray sighed. She hated
the thought of other
Weatherlings being scared
of her magic. 'Sure, my magic

is a bit different,' she said. 'But that doesn't make it *scary*. Instead of making pretty clouds using a curly cloud-crook like Drift, I use my staff to make colourful rainbows.' Ray pulled out her long golden staff, which was held to the back of her waistcoat by two hand-stitched straps courtesy of Snowden's excellent sewing skills.

'What do rainbows do?' asked Flow, shuffling forward a little while Drift climbed on to Ray's lap, her eyes wide with excitement.

'Well, I can use my magic to control someone else's weather,' said Ray. 'So, it's kind of like having ALL the weather magic! But it's also really handy when there's a Rogue around . . . you know about Rogues, don't you?'

Drift and Flow nodded furiously.

'Rogues are *naughty*. And they make BAD weather like TORNADOES and scary LIGHTNING and hailstones the size of ME!' Drift blurted out.

'Exactly,' Ray said. 'Earth's weather is carefully planned by the Council of Forecasters, but the Rogues mess this up. So, I can use my rainbows to take control of a Rogue's naughty weather and turn it into something good.' Ray paused. 'Well, once I'm fully trained anyway.'

'That's lovely,' said Drift with a big smile. She turned to her friend. 'See, I told you Ray wasn't scary.'

'But if rainbows are so good, why haven't we ever seen any before?' asked Flow.

'The Weatherlands *used* to have lots of rainbow weather magic,' said Ray. 'But a long time ago, the most TERRIBLE Rogue took it all away. Her name was Tornadia Twist.'

Drift gasped and Flow yelped before making a windy TOOT that definitely *wasn't* magic.

'My mum's spoken about her!' whispered Drift. 'But why was she so bad? And how did the rainbow magic end up with you?'

Ray shuddered even though it was warm outside. Tornadia was one of the most dangerous Rogues in weather history, and also the reason why Ray had been born with no magic at all.

Ray moved a little closer to the young Weatherlings. 'Tornadia used to be a Rainbow Weatherling too,' she said, keeping her voice low. 'But she decided to use her power for BAD. Tornadia banded together with other Rogues to create a HUGE storm that lasted for a hundred years.'

'That's HORRIBLE!' cried Drift, hugging her cloud-owl to her chest. Flow hadn't blinked once, hanging on to Ray's every word.

Ray continued. 'On the night of an Eclipse over a thousand years ago, when she knew the Rainbow Weatherlings would be dancing around the Oldest Tree in the World, Tornadia *destroyed* the tree. It released a substance called Shadow Essence, which ABSORBED *all* the rainbow weather magic and turned it into a big black lump of crystal.'

The children's mouths gaped open and their eyes were the size of plates.

'As centuries passed, rainbows were slowly forgotten. But then I found the crystal and

released the trapped magic!' Ray finished
with a grin. Nim miaowed joyfully.

Snowden leaned towards the little
Weatherlings, a long line of think-flakes
pouring from his left ear. 'Ray triggered the
crystal because she is a TRUE descendant of
the long-lost Rainbow Weatherling clan.'

'I want to see your rainbow weather magic!'
cried Flow.

Ray screwed up her nose, then grinned.
'Oh, all right. But only a LITTLE bit!'

Drift and Flow cheered. The rest of the adults
at the party were so busy chatting, Ray was sure
she'd get away with one little trick. What could
possibly go wrong . . .?

CHAPTER 2
POOF!

Ray checked that Aunt Foggaleena was out of sight and made sure her parents were still busy chatting on the other side of the puff pod patch. Then she gripped her staff and got herself into position.

'What are you going to doooo?!' asked Drift, barely able to contain her excitement.

'Hmm, I'm wondering what rainbow gift I can use?' Ray pondered. 'I don't know very many, yet . . .'

'Rainbow gift?' said Drift. 'Like a present?'

Ray chuckled. 'Not quite. As well as being able to take control of someone else's magic, I can do other things too, such as making rainbow slides, OR creating big rainbow bubbles.

Those are rainbow gifts. Last week I learned to SHRINK weather!'

Drift gasped. 'Oooh! Could you make our cloud-creatures really tiny and cute?'

Her cloud-owl hooted in agreement. Flow was jumping up and down on the spot swinging her wind instrument around with joy.

Ray thought hard. 'I've only practised that gift once on Nim,' she said. 'And it seemed to work fine . . . so I *guess* I could give it another go!'

Ray had spent lots of time over the past few weeks learning about all the different types of rainbow gifts. Every Rainbow Weatherling that had ever lived was born with one additional ability called a *rainbow gift*. They were usually named after their gift.

Ray enjoyed looking at all the different names of the ancient Weatherlings and trying to guess what each of their gifts could do. *Rainbow Slide* had created long bands of colour to transport herself from one location to another. *Rainbow Rewind* had used his gift to turn back the weather by one minute – handy for avoiding a nasty lightning zap from a Rogue!

The one that intrigued Ray the most was *Professor Rainbow Beard's* gift. Ray wondered how above earth *beards* had anything to do with rainbows or the weather. What could his gift do? She was sure she'd find out one day.

No two Rainbow Weatherlings had the same gift, and if the Rainbow Weatherlings hadn't have been made extinct, then Ray would have had her own gift too (she often wondered what this would have been!). But when Ray had destroyed the shadow crystal, she received the WHOLE CLAN's rainbow weather magic, which meant Ray didn't just have ONE gift – she had them ALL. And this meant she had LOTS to learn!

Drift and Flow were watching her intently. Ray tried to remember how to perform the weather shrinking gift. Something about moving her staff around in a big circle? And making the circular motions smaller and smaller?

Ray held her staff out and felt the familiar

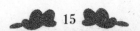

tingle in her fingertips as her rainbow weather magic flooded through her. She began to swirl the staff around. Ray let out a sigh of relief as a beautiful stream of colours poured from the top of the staff. The children oohed and ahhed, smiles spreading across their faces. (It was hard NOT to smile when you saw a rainbow, after all!)

The colours wove their way silently around every cloud-creature at the party. Then Ray made the circular motions smaller. Slowly but surely, the cloud-creatures in her magical grip began to get smaller too. It was working!

Drift and Flow burst into fits of giggles. The chattering adults didn't seem to notice.

'Aww, you've made my cloud-owl look SO cute!' said Drift, holding her now teeny-tiny cloud-owl in the palm of her hand.

'I wish *I* had rainbow weather magic,' said Flow.

Ray was relieved her little trick had gone to plan. But then her fingers fizzled furiously and she felt her magic stutter.

'Uh-oh . . .' Ray muttered.

The cloud-creatures began to wibble and wobble, before expanding outwards at super speed.

'Ray?' said Snowden. 'What's happening?'

Ray swung her staff around desperately. 'I think I tried to use my magic on too many cloud-creatures at once!' she said.

The adults *definitely* noticed now as their cloud-creatures began to get bigger and bigger and BIGGER. Then . . .

POOF!

Every single cloud-creature at the party exploded.

The children screamed.

Nim, on the other hand, was LOVING every second of seeing the other cloud-creatures explode just like him. His HUGE floofy body spun joyfully around in circles before getting tangled up in his own limbs.

'No need to panic!' Ray urged, even though her mind was in a whirlwind. 'Everything's under control!'

'EVERYTHING'S OUT OF CONTROL!' screeched Aunt Foggaleena, running through the crowd in a frenzy.

'It's OK, I can make it right again!' said Ray, holding her staff up. 'I can try another rainbow gift I learned! This one rewinds weather by one minute.'

She pointed her rainbow staff towards the jumble of cloudy wisps where the cloud-creatures had once been, and closed her eyes.

'Are you sure about this, Ray?' squeaked Snowden.

'I've got this,' said Ray, though her heart was thudding in her chest. She closed her eyes. 'I just need to replay what happened in my head, but *backwards* . . .'

Bracing her staff tightly, she imagined all the cloud-creatures coming together whole again – full and floofy with their heads intact.

Ray dragged her staff backwards as if pulling a huge lever. She felt the familiar tingle in her fingers as a rush of colours filled her mind. Then she heard more screams.

'Did it work?!' said Ray, opening her eyes.

POOF! POOF! POOF! POOF! POOF!

The cloud-creatures kept reforming then exploding over and over, AGAIN and AGAIN.

'Oh. I don't think that worked,' said Ray.

'They're exploding on repeat!' cried Snowden, narrowly missing a cloud-cow's udders soaring past his head.

Foggaleena pointed a shaky finger at Ray. 'This is YOUR doing, isn't it!' she spat.

'It was an accident!' cried Ray. 'But don't worry, the cloud-creatures will be back

 20

to normal soon. Nim explodes ALL the time, and he's completely fine.'

Nim's head floated past slowly with his paws attached to it.

'See?' Ray tried to smile at her aunt. 'Completely *fine*.'

But Aunt Foggaleena looked as though SHE might explode in a minute.

'Ray? I'm going to guess this has something to do with you!'

Ray's mum, Cloudia Grey, appeared with her hands on her hips. Her large grey hair was piled high on her head with various objects protruding from it. A reel of silver lining was attached to her belt. She looked cross. Ray's dad was right behind her, along with his grumpy cloud-whale Waldo. Waldo looked even grumpier than usual, having just exploded for a third time in a row.

'Well, I may have had something to do with it,' Ray started. 'But –'

'Ray has CURSED ALL THE CLOUD-CREATURES!' interrupted Aunt Foggaleena

21

wildly, before running back into the crowd.

Aunt Foggaleena LOVED to overreact. Cloudia rolled her eyes. 'Now, Ray-Ray,' she said. 'Tell us exactly what happened.'

'It was an accident, honest,' said Ray. 'I was showing Drift and Flow my magic and tried to perform the gift to make the cloud-creatures small and cute, but I haven't really practised it properly . . .' She trailed off.

'Oh, Ray, you know you've not mastered all the rainbow gifts yet,' said Cloudia sternly.

Ray sighed. 'Yeah, it all went a bit wrong. I'm sorry,' she said.

'I know.' Cloudia tapped Ray's nose. 'But go and apologise to your aunt anyway. We all know she can be a right fog-goblin, but we need to keep the peace today. It IS baby Cloudiculus's first birthday, after all.'

'I guess,' said Ray with a wonky smile.

Ray's dad, Haze, gave Ray a kindly pat on the shoulder. 'We'd best go and help everyone find the rest of their cloud-creatures and sort out their

limbs,' he said, pointing his cloud-crook towards Waldo, who was now just a cloud-whale tail.

'Snowden and I will help,' said Ray. 'I've had good practice searching for bits of Nim over the years.'

'On it!' said Snowden. 'I'll just finish my drizzle-pickle sandwich.' He was about to take the last bite when . . .

SPLOSH!

An almighty wave of rainwater covered Snowden from head to toe, just missing Ray.

'Droplett's arrived,' Snowden said flatly, wiping the water from his eyes. 'And, as usual, the rest of my sandwich is ruined.'

A spiky-haired girl emerged from a puddle in front of Snowden. Droplett Dewbells was Ray's other best friend. She was as feisty as Snowden was calm. Anyone who dared mess with Droplett or her friends got a good splosh in the bottom.

Unfortunately for Snowden, it was always his drizzle-pickle sandwich that got a good splosh whenever Droplett turned up. The soggy sandwich fell to the floor, but Nim soon floated along to lap up the remains.

'Sorry I'm late to the piff paff party!' said Droplett with a grin. 'Are you all having fun?'

A child ran past screaming, followed by a cloud-bear's head with beaks for eyes.

Ray bit her lip. 'Hmm,' she said. 'It depends on your definition of *fun* . . .'

CHAPTER 3
THE HEAD OF BUMS

It took a good hour to put all the cloud-creatures back together, and Ray was pretty sure a few of them still had the wrong limbs. But she decided it was best not to say anything about that right now.

'I'm sorry, Aunty,' said Ray sheepishly. 'My magic is still really new to me, but I'm trying my best to learn.'

'Ray meant no harm,' Cloudia added. She glanced at her daughter, eyebrows raised. 'She will be more careful next time.'

'There won't BE a next time,' hissed Foggaleena with a dark glare. 'Because Ray is uninvited to ALL future puff pod parties!'

Foggaleena picked up little Cloudiculus

and turned to the crowd. 'EVERYONE!' she cried. 'Gather round! It's FINALLY time for the ceremonial picking!'

'Count yourself lucky, Ray-Ray,' Cloudia whispered as they made their way over to the puff pod patch. 'I wish I had an excuse not to come to these parties. But since Foggaleena is your dad's sister, I kind of have to!'

Ray, Droplett and Snowden stood on a tree stump at the back of the crowd, next to Cloudia and Haze. Nim sat on Ray's head.

Aunt Foggaleena cleared her throat loudly. 'As you know, my darling Cloudiculus Von Fluff turns ONE today, and I am delighted to have MOST of you here . . .' she shot a glare towards Ray, '. . . to watch the special moment where we reveal his cloud-creature for life.'

Ray felt her mind drifting as Foggaleena droned on and on about how wonderful Cloudiculus was – when something suddenly caught her attention. There was a pretty etching on one of the tree trunks next to the puff pod patch. It looked a bit like a swirly eye, and it was glowing brightly. She'd visited this spot in the forest many times but hadn't noticed it before.

'Looks like the Sky Scrawlers have been here,' whispered Ray to her friends, pointing to the decorative scribble. Sky Scrawlers were notorious for writing or drawing strange symbols on buildings and walls around the City of Celestia.

Snowden adjusted his glasses and squinted. 'Where? I can't see anything.'

'Me neither,' said Droplett, standing on her tiptoes.

'Can't you see it? Right there on the tree trunk,' said Ray, pointing again.

'HUSH, EVERYONE!' Foggaleena cried, making the friends jump and turn back to the puff pod patch. Cloudiculus was sitting on the ground, chewing on the stem of one of the pearly plants. 'A pod has been chosen!'

Aunt Foggaleena plucked the puff pod from the ground. The petals slowly opened. The party of Weatherlings waited for the light and satisfying

29

POOF of a baby cloud-creature to appear. But there was no poof at all. The puff pod was completely empty.

'That's weird,' whispered Ray.

'I don't understand,' Aunt Foggaleena shrieked. 'WHERE IS THE BABY CLOUD-CREATURE?! Without a cloud-creature, Cloudiculus won't be able to use his magic!'

'Maybe it's REALLY tiny? Like a cloud-hummingbird?' Ray suggested.

But there was no sign of even a tiny creature.

'It must be a dud pod,' Haze suggested with a forced, jolly smile. 'Try another one?'

Cloudiculus poked at another puff pod. Foggaleena plucked it from the ground. The petals opened. Nothing.

The crowd went quiet. Baby Cloudiculus burst out laughing, then rolled on to his back and farted. The sound echoed through the silent forest and the pong that followed parted the crowd.

'Third time lucky?' said Haze, his smile fading.

Cloudiculus sneezed on another pod. Foggaleena pulled it out from the ground. The puff pod opened . . . but again, nothing.

'Where are all the baby clouds?' cried Aunt Foggaleena.

'I'm sure there's a perfectly good explanation,' said Haze. The crowd waited. He cleared his throat. 'I, er, have no explanation.'

'Someone call a cloud professional right away!' shouted Foggaleena.

Everyone sat around, getting bored. Nim sniffed at the empty pods and exploded with a bang. Then they all heard a very loud and operatic voice.

'I HAVE ARRIVED, MY DARLINGS!'

A woman pushed her way through the crowd, twirling her cloud-crook merrily. She was wearing a VERY extravagant wide-brimmed hat, bright lipstick and three pairs of pink-tinted glasses. Her long, dark purple coat had the tallest collars Ray had ever seen. A large and miserable-looking cloud-slug followed her.

'I am HERE to solve your cloudy conundrum!' she trilled.

'Now she has STYLE,' said Snowden, watching as the woman began to hand out business cards to everyone at the party. 'And her hat seems familiar,' he added thoughtfully.

Ray stared at the four letters printed across the front of the business card. They didn't spell a word she'd expected on a grown-up business card. Were the letters getting jumbled up in her head, like they usually did?

'Do not fear, my darlings,' declared the woman. 'I am Agent Nephia Weatherwart. This is my cloud-slug, Mr Steve.'

Mr Steve remained emotionless.

'And I am the head of B.U.M.S.,' the woman said.

Ray *had* seen the letters right. She tried not to laugh.

'Head of *BUMS*?' snorted Droplett.

'The Bureau of Unexplained Meteorological Sightings,' Agent Nephia replied. 'B.U.M.S. for short. A secret organisation for investigating and explaining the unexplained within the Weatherlands. I know everything there is to know about cloud equations and cloudulations. Surely you've read my book *Cloudy Conundrums and Other Overcast Illnesses*?'

The crowd was silent.

Snowden's ears began pouring with think-flakes. 'How have I NOT read that book? I've read EVERY book in the sky,' he said.

B . U . M . S

'I know the ins and outs of puff pods,' Agent Nephia continued, crouching down next to the empty pods. She chuckled to herself. 'But I must say, I've never heard of a puff pod being EMPTY. This is quite the puff pod predicament!'

The secret weather agent sat for a long time studying the empty pods, while Aunt Foggaleena stood over her like an annoying shadow.

'Does anyone have a magnifying glass?' asked Agent Nephia suddenly.

'Yes!' said Ray's mum, reaching into her mop of hair and pulling out a boot. 'Oh,' she said, looking at the boot in surprise. 'I've been looking for that everywhere. Hang on, it's in here somewhere . . .' Cloudia managed to extract three odd socks, a forgotten sandwich and a decorated bowl before finally producing a magnifying glass.

There were five minutes of tense waiting while the detective studied the empty pods. Then she got to her feet.

'WELL?' demanded Aunt Foggaleena. 'What's the verdict?'

'The empty puff pods are perfectly healthy,' said Nephia, stroking her chin thoughtfully. 'But I shall perform ONE more test on the rest of the unopened pods to determine whether there are any baby clouds inside.'

Agent Nephia sniffed another pod and pulled a funny face, before closing her eyes and lifting her hands above her head.

'To learn about the pod, I must BE the pod,' she announced.

Ray had to hold her mouth to stop herself from bursting into giggles.

'Are you SURE you can tell whether they're empty by doing that?' said Foggaleena.

Nephia put up a hand to silence her. 'Hush while I channel my INNER pod.'

Ray really hoped the rest of the pods had baby clouds inside. She went to hug Nim for comfort, but he still hadn't returned from his last explosion.

Agent Nephia finally got to her feet. 'I do believe that every puff pod in the patch is indeed EMPTY.'

There were gasps from the crowd.

'WHAT SHALL I DO?' shrieked Foggaleena. 'My darling Cloudiculus won't be able to use his magic until he has bonded to a cloud-creature!' Then she fainted, along with her tiny cloud-sparrow.

'Agent Nephia, why are the puff pods empty?' asked Ray, her tummy filled with dread. 'Is there something you can do?'

'I've never ever seen anything like this before,' said Agent Nephia, shaking her head. 'My brilliant brain is stumped.'

'I'm going to call the Council of Forecasters,' said Cloudia, opening the lid of her Compass Caller. 'We must report this!'

While they waited for the Council of Forecasters to arrive, Ray's dad wafted a huge, fully charged lightning leaf across Aunt Foggaleena's face. When the lightning leaf had zapped her between the eyes a few times, she eventually came round.

'There, there,' said Haze, helping his sister up, her cloud-sparrow squished under her armpit.

Foggaleena turned to glare at Ray. 'My poor baby won't have a cloud-creature, and it's all YOUR fault!'

'How is this MY fault?' said Ray with a frown.

'You must have done something to the puff pods when you made our cloud-creatures *explode* earlier on,' Aunt Foggaleena cried. 'Everything was fine before you started messing around with your *rainbows*.' She said the words 'rainbows' as if it left a bad taste in her mouth. 'What if you made all the baby clouds disappear FOREVER?'

'That can't be true!' Ray retorted.

But a teeny-weeny feeling of doubt was creeping into her mind.

What if she *had* somehow caused the baby clouds to vanish?

CHAPTER 4

THE RAINBURROW

'Ray's magic is NOT responsible for the empty pods,' Cloudia snapped.

'How can you be sure?' barked Aunt Foggaleena.

Cloudia glared at Foggaleena. 'Because I'm Ray's mum,' she said. 'Ray's magic is good. She would never do anything like that on purpose.'

Ray's heart swelled. Her mum was the BEST.

Thankfully the Council of Forecasters arrived and everyone was told to go home. The puff pod party was well and truly over. Ray watched as a Snow Forecaster used his weather magic to create an icy fence around the puff pod patch, while Agent Nephia discussed her findings with the rest of the council.

Ray and her friends slowly left the forest,

41

with Ray twiddling her blue streak of hair.

'Ray, you're worrying,' said Snowden, putting an arm around her shoulder.

'How can you tell?' asked Ray, puffing out her chest and giving a strained smile. 'I'm FINE!'

'You're a terrible liar,' said Snowden. 'You *always* twiddle your blue streak of hair when you're worried. And you pull at your green hair when you're telling a fib!' He gave Ray a lopsided smile, revealing a dimple in one cheek.

'Snow-boy's right,' said Droplett, helping Ray unravel the tangled hair from around her fingers. 'What's up?'

Ray took a deep breath. 'What if I *did* accidentally do something to the puff pods?' she said. 'Nobody really knows how rainbow weather magic affects things.'

There was a sound like someone blowing up a balloon as Nim finally reappeared. He was wearing a very confused expression and his head was far too small for his body, but Ray didn't care. All she wanted was a BIG cloud-cat cuddle.

Nim nuzzled into her neck and then licked at her cheeks, making her feel a little better.

'We don't think it's your fault,' said Snowden gently. 'But even if it somehow is, then we know you'll work out how to make it all better again. And we'll be there to help.'

Ray's lips twitched and suddenly she found herself smiling. 'You're right, Snowden,' she said, straightening up. 'I'm not just a Rainbow Weatherling. I'm RAY GREY, and Ray Grey *never* gives up. I'm going to help find those baby clouds, no matter what it takes!'

She high-fived her friends and completely missed on both attempts. Nim miaowed happily.

'Let's go to the Rainburrow,' Ray said. 'There MUST be answers there about how rainbow weather magic affects clouds and puff pods.'

Ray and her friends headed to their new favourite hangout. Nim floated alongside Ray, occasionally spinning in the air and catching Snowpogglian

Dalooloo bugs in his mouth.

The leaves of the surrounding trees shimmered in the light of the great Sunflower in the sky, casting patterns on the seven standing stones in the Weatherstone Circle. It was always sunny in the Weatherlands, thanks to the glowing Sunflower, which gave Earth its warmth and light.

The Weatherstone Circle had always been one of Ray's favourite places. Each of the seven standing stones was carved with a unique symbol showing a type of weather and the

instrument used to channel it, such as snow gloves
for snow magic, or a rain cape for rain magic.
There had once been only six Weatherstones,
but when Ray had received her rainbow weather
magic, the tree that had stood at the centre of the
circle disappeared, revealing the biggest standing
stone of all – the Rainbow Weatherstone.

Ray stood by the Rainbow Weatherstone and
called out the password.

'BEARD!' she cried.

A swirly rainbow doorway appeared, allowing
Ray and her friends to step right through the

stone, shoot down a rainbow slide and end up under the ground below.

Inside the underground burrow – the Rainburrow – curly tree roots lined the walls and sparkly sunflower lanterns glittered as wind chimes jingled lightly. Over a thousand years ago, this had been home to Ray's ancient ancestor, Professor Rainbow Beard. The Rainburrow was the PERFECT place for Ray to practise her magic every afternoon. All the notes left by Professor Rainbow Beard detailing how rainbow weather magic worked were *very* useful, even though there was a lot of them to get through. And it was just as well, because the Sky Academy didn't have any lessons for rainbow weather magic.

For the past six months the Rainburrow had also been home to La Blaze DeLight,

a Sun Weatherling. The tall, crystal-eyed woman appeared when Ray and her friends arrived.

'Hi, kids, LOOK! I made some sunflower skates over the weekend,' La Blaze exclaimed, pointing to her glowing feet with a grin. 'They're powered by sun magic! I can't wait until I'm allowed to go outside again, so I can try them out properly.' She rolled backwards. 'Just don't look behind that poster . . .'

A clumsily drawn picture of a sunflower peeled off the wall to reveal a La Blaze-shaped hole.

'I WILL fix that,' La Blaze added sheepishly, rubbing her forehead, which had a bit of a bump.

La Blaze had to stay inside the Rainburrow for a year, as punishment for almost destroying the world's oldest forest. La Blaze had always been Ray's hero, so when she found out the Sun Weatherling had turned Rogue, it had been a kick in the stomach. But Ray knew La Blaze had good inside her, and she was right. The Sun Weatherling really had turned over a new leaf, and was VERY good at organising all of Professor

Rainbow Beard's ancient books and scribbles
ready for Ray's rainbow magic practice.

While Snowden sifted through a large book on
rainbow magic lore, trying to learn how rainbow
weather magic might affect cloud-creatures, Ray
updated La Blaze on the events of the puff pod
party. Droplett and Nim made themselves useful
by quickly eating a batch of bright blue cakes
called rumblebuns (if you didn't eat them quickly,
the top exploded with a bright pink goo!).

'Sounds like an eventful day,' said La Blaze.
She tapped her chin, then widened her eyes.
'Oooh! There MIGHT be one gift that could help
you find the baby clouds.'

Ray's heart fluttered. 'Really? Which one?'

'Well, you don't know WHERE the baby
clouds are, right?' said La Blaze. 'They COULD
be lost or hiding . . .'

She picked up a pile of papers, each detailing
a Rainbow Weatherling and what they could do.

'This lady was called *Rainbow Retrieve*!'
said La Blaze, tapping a picture of the ancient

Weatherling. 'Her gift gave her the ability to find lost or hidden weather.'

Ray felt her heart fill with hope. 'La Blaze, you're a GENIUS! Now I just have to learn it.'

Ray braced her staff. 'If this works, we'll be able find the baby clouds,' she said, hopping up and down with excitement.

'But what if the baby clouds aren't actually lost *or* hidden?' asked Snowden. 'What if they've disappeared altogether?'

'I guess there's nothing to lose,' said Ray. She grinned. 'And if there IS, then I'll find it!'

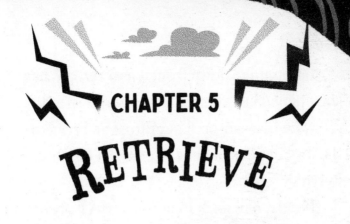

CHAPTER 5

RETRIEVE

'Let's practise in the Rainburrow first,' said La
Blaze. 'Just in case you retrieve something you
don't want to!'

'Good idea,' said Ray, twirling her staff round
in her hand. 'Then we can all go to the puff pod
patch to find the baby clouds for real!'

La Blaze shook her head. 'Sorry, kid,' she
said. 'I have to stay here. If I'm caught outside
the Rainburrow, I'll get sent to Precipitory Prison
for good.'

Ray pulled a face. 'Good point. OK, let's
practise. I'm sure it's not THAT hard. Nim can
be my test subject.' She gave the floofy feline a
pat on the head. Nim spun happily. 'I'll close my
eyes while Nim hides.'

Ray counted down from ten to zero. When she opened her eyes, Nim was nowhere to be seen. La Blaze cleared her throat and read out the instructions on how to perform Rainbow Retrieve's gift.

'Firstly, one must focus on WHAT needs to be found,' said La Blaze.

Ray thought only of Nim, his big, fluffy cloud face filling her mind. It was lovely.

'Once your focus is entirely on the lost or hidden thing, you point your staff upwards,' finished La Blaze.

Ray concentrated hard. Nim, Nim, Nim, Nim, she thought. But then her mind began to wander, as it did a lot. La Blaze's words echoed in her head: *Just in case you retrieve something you really don't want to . . .* She didn't want fog goblins – they were awful – but there wasn't anything else THAT bad in the surrounding forest . . .

'Ray?' said Snowden's voice, snapping her out of her wandering thoughts.

'Oh. Ready!' she said, coming back with a start and pointing her staff upwards.

She felt the warmth of her magic filling her up. The colours rushed through her mind. She held her staff tight as a thin rainbow poured from its top, creating a colourful trail that wove around the Rainburrow, through the root-covered walls and out into the forest.

Ray felt a tug on her staff as if something was pulling on the end of the long, wispy rainbow. 'Yes!' she cried in delight. 'I've caught Nim!'

Something appeared with a POP at Ray's feet. A thick, stinky green fog began to fill the space.

'I don't think that's Nim,' said Snowden, covering his nose.

There was a giggling and gurgling sound. Ray caught sight of something running around her feet with a spotty bottom.

'I think you found a lost baby fog goblin!' said La Blaze, coughing as her face disappeared behind the green mist.

It took a good hour to catch the baby fog

goblin and for the stinky fog to subside. Nim
reappeared to help. Droplett puddle-ported the
forest pest outside back to the underground
boglins, where it belonged.

Ray slumped on to the floor, letting her
rainbow staff drop beside her. 'Sorry about that,'
she sighed. 'I thought about how I DIDN'T want
to find any fog goblins, and that made me find one
. . . Billowing breezes, my magic is HARD.'

'You'll get there,' said La Blaze, putting an
arm around Ray's shoulders. 'Be patient. You've
got ten years of catching up to do. Everyone else
was born with magic, remember?'

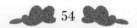

'And not to mention the fact you've got a whole clan's worth of rainbow gifts to learn! That's a LOT of magic inside of you,' Droplett added.

'You're right,' said Ray. She smiled a little wearily at La Blaze. 'Don't get me wrong, I am SO grateful for all your help with my rainbow learning. But I could really do with another Rainbow Weatherling around. At least they'd understand how this magic works.'

The sundial on the wall dinged.

Ray gasped. 'How is it that time already? We have to get back to Cloud Nine for dinner.' She got to her feet and tucked her staff back into the holders on her waistcoat. 'I'll be back tomorrow afternoon,' she told La Blaze. 'We'll look for another way to solve this puff pod mystery. I am determined to find out what's happened to the baby clouds!'

Outside the Rainburrow, Ray and her friends jumped on Nim's floofy back and took to the skies. Ray couldn't stop thinking about the empty puff pods as they flew over the Forest of Fahrenheits and across the City of Celestia.

The city was always busy with Wind Weatherlings surfing on their various trumpets and horns and flutes. Lightning sizzled and thunder rumbled gently as a Thunder 'n' Lightning Weatherling duo (they always came in twos) prepared for a performance of their newest Sky Shanty on Crackle Corner. Ray breathed in the sweet scents of sizzling snowflake slices and tasty rumblebuns as they flew over the Rising Bun Bakery, before soaring towards the Cloudimulus Suburbs.

'Do you guys want to come back to my house for Dad's biosphere burgers?' asked Ray.

'ALWAYS!' sang Droplett, rubbing her tummy.

'I can't,' said Snowden. 'I have to get home to prepare for the Annual Greatest Snowman Gathering tomorrow.

Granny Everfreeze is making a brand-new hat for the occasion.'

'Hold on, snow-it-all. It's a school day tomorrow,' said Droplett.

'I won't be in school tomorrow,' Snowden replied.

Ray and Droplett looked at their friend in disbelief.

'You've never *ever* missed school,' said Ray. 'Not even when you had icicles hanging from your nose. Your attendance is one hundred per cent.'

'One hundred and TWO actually,' Snowden corrected. 'But the Annual Greatest Snowman Gathering is a tradition for every Snow Weatherling aged eleven and over. It'll be my first time. We visit the LONGEST STANDING snowman in the world. It hasn't melted in over a thousand years!'

'I read about that snowman in one of La Blaze's books,' gasped Ray.

'That seems . . . *impossible*! How has it not melted yet?' shrieked Droplett.

Snowden shrugged. 'Nobody knows. It's very close to where the Oldest Tree in the World once was. Centuries ago, Snow Weatherlings believed it was lucky, and named it the Greatest Snowman. It became a tradition that on the first night of winter every year, they'd visit the snowman to leave offerings of thanks, cast ancient spells together and add more snow to it.' He smiled wistfully. 'Granny Everfreeze makes the FANCIEST hat as our offering every year, just like her gran did and her gran before that. It's an Everfreeze tradition, which I hope to carry on.'

'Sounds like the Greatest AND the Best-Dressed Snowman around!' giggled Ray.

'Well count yourself lucky, snow-boy,' said Droplett. 'We have morning assembly tomorrow, then DOUBLE Thermomoteering with Mr Current. Worst day EVER.'

PUFF POD PALAVER

Weekly Weatherval

CHAPTER 6

A PUFF POD PALAVER

Early on Monday morning, Ray was woken up
by the muttering of naughty words from the roof
as her mum hammered her finger or got her
hair caught while replacing the silver lining on
Cloud Nine.

The empty puff pod news was already all
over the *Weekly Weathervane*. Postman Puff
delivered the newspaper through the window and
straight into Ray's bowl of foggy frostflakes with a
SPLASH. Luckily Nim lapped up the milk before
it got too soggy.

'Thanks, Nim,' said Ray, giving the cloud-cat
a kiss on the head. She picked up the newspaper,
and carefully read the words:

PUFF POD PALAVER!

*Following a puff pod picking party
yesterday afternoon, the Council of
Forecasters have confirmed that the baby
clouds inside the puff pods are MISSING.
Agent Nephia Weatherwart added that
each pod seemed perfectly healthy.
Therefore, we believe there may be more
to this situation than meets the eye.
When interviewed, Cloud Weatherling
Foggaleena Von Fluff was very
distressed. 'My baby has been denied
his life companion, and consequently his
magic. I don't think it's a coincidence that
this should happen straight after Ray
Grey made everyone's cloud-creature
explode.'*

Ray frowned. 'I can't believe my own aunt would
blame me like this,' she said.

Nim hissed at the page. Ray continued to read:

*The Council of Forecasters has urged
Weatherlings not to panic. Head
Forecaster Flurryweather Floatatious
assures us, 'We have the situation under
control and have deployed our top
Forecasters, Weather Warriors, doctors
and detectives to try to get to the bottom
of the situation and find the missing baby
clouds as soon as possible.'*

Ray hugged Nim closer to her. She thought of
her cousin, Cloudiculus. What would happen if
he never got a cloud-companion? Would he be
without cloud magic forever?

'PUMPKIN!' Ray's dad shouted.

Ray jumped and Nim's face fell off.

'Dad!' cried Ray, holding her heart. She'd
completely forgotten he had been sitting at the
breakfast table this whole time. He was sipping at
a cup of ozonian tea, engrossed in a book called

Oh My Gourds.

'Ooh, sorry Ray-Ray,' he said sheepishly. 'I got knocked out by this book during a book-nado weather battle in London last month.' He stroked the page affectionately.

Haze Grey was a Weather Warrior. He fought Weather Rogues, who created storms on Earth. But no matter how bad the Rogue, or how big the storm, Haze ALWAYS made sure to collect interesting facts and objects he found along the way. A few weeks back, he'd brought home something called a 'yo-yo' which had blown Ray's MIND.

'Did you know that on Earth they grow these funny plump orange things called pumpkins?' Haze told Ray. 'And every year on a special occasion called . . .' he checked back at the page he was reading, '*Halloweeeen* – they carve pictures into them?'

'Weird,' said Ray. She was usually more curious about her dad's interesting facts, but she was feeling too distracted. She twiddled a strand

of blue hair. 'Dad, do you think I made the baby
clouds disappear?'

'Oh, Ray-Ray.' Haze put an arm around his
daughter and gave her a light squeeze. 'Nobody
knows what has happened to the baby clouds. But
I don't think it's anything to do with you or your
weather magic. Everything will be right as rain,
you'll see! And speaking of rain, I'd best get to
work.' He checked the Compass Caller attached
to his waistcoat pocket. 'There's a strange
downpour in England . . .'

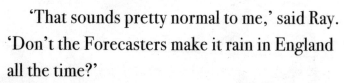

'That sounds pretty normal to me,' said Ray. 'Don't the Forecasters make it rain in England all the time?'

'Indeed. But this particular rainfall *wasn't* planned by the Council of Forecasters,' Haze replied. 'We have no idea who is creating it!'

'That *is* odd,' said Ray. 'Well, good luck finding the mysterious rainmaker!' And she waved goodbye to her dad as he left Cloud Nine on the back of Waldo, his cloud-whale.

Ray's books and rainbow notes went flying as she rolled full speed through the Sky Academy entrance, thanks to Nim exploding just before they landed. Most of the other students dived out of the way in time. They were used to Nim's crash landings by now.

Sky Academy was a higgledy-piggledy building, decorated with turrets and twisting stairs that connected the many levels of the weather school. Thick branches curled themselves in and around the structure, making it as much a

part of the forest as the trees.

Ray gathered everything up, then clambered her way to the very top level of the school for their Monday morning assembly. Lining up with the rest of the first years, she couldn't help noticing the stares and hushed whispers as she passed.

Ray felt a tap on her shoulder. She turned to see a fellow first year, Percy Wonderwhoosh. He didn't even wait to say hello before chattering away at full speed.

'Did you see the *Weekly Weathervane* this morning, Ray? What was it like when you saw the EMPTY puff pods? Was it strange? Must've been sad. Was it SCARY? I don't think you did it. I think it's gotta be a CLOUD-NAPPER! Don't you think?!' A small TOOT of wind magic erupted from the trumpet strapped to his back.

'If it IS a cloud-napper, I'll totally SPLOSH 'em!' said Droplett, appearing dramatically from a puddle behind them.

More students joined the line, sneaking glances at Ray. She'd never been so eager for

assembly to start.

'Do you think a ROGUE took the baby clouds?' asked Percy.

'I'm not sure,' Ray replied, wishing Percy would stop talking about it in front of all the other students. 'But hopefully we can all work together to find the baby clouds and bring them safely home. I really hope they are OK.'

'Pah, what rubbish, don't believe Ray!'

'She doesn't care whether the clouds are OK!'

Ray sighed. There were only two Weatherlings who spoke in nasty rhymes like that.

Frazzle and Fump Striker, the Thunder 'n' Lightning twins.

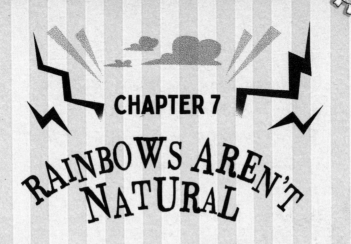

CHAPTER 7

RAINBOWS AREN'T NATURAL

Frazzle and Fump were the meanest kids in school. They had teased Ray before she had weather magic and were even *worse* now that she did. Droplett growled and grabbed at the edge of her rain cape, poised for sploshing.

'I DO care about the clouds,' said Ray, feeling her temper flare. 'I care about ALL the weather.'

The twins stood side by side, their green streaked fringes swept across their grinning faces.

'*We heard your rainbow magic went wrong,*' said Frazzle.

'*And THAT'S why the baby clouds are gone!*' finished Fump.

Ray tried to ignore the mean pair. But they carried on regardless.

'We can't trust you, your magic is WEIRD!' said Frazzle, twirling her lightning stick between her fingers.

'Rainbows aren't natural, they should be FEARED!' added Fump.

Ray put on her glariest glare. 'You're wrong,' she said firmly. 'Rainbow Weatherlings exist to keep balance and harmony between Earth and sky. And that's exactly what I'll do.'

Frazzle and Fump cackled.

'And in case you'd forgotten, Ray saved us all from a load of Rogues a few months ago!' said Droplett. 'I don't see either of YOU doing that in your first term at school.'

Ray smiled at her friend.

Frazzle tilted her head to one side. Small crackles of green electricity zip-zapped from her lightning stick. Fump chortled and bomped the thunder drum strapped to his back, creating a low rumble through the corridor.

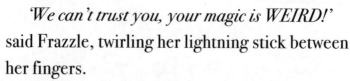

Frazzle leaned forward. *'We have our suspicions, 'cos what are the ODDS . . .'*

'That YOU'RE the one who emptied the PODS!' finished Frazzle.

Droplett got ready to splosh. Then, to Ray's surprise, Percy grabbed his wind trumpet and held it shakily to his mouth.

'Stop being so horrible to Ray,' he stammered at the twins. 'Or else I'll let out WIND right in your faces!'

All the students erupted with giggles.

Taking the opportunity while they had everybody's attention, Frazzle chimed in a purposefully loud voice: *'Ray once took control of MY lightning.'*

'It's TRUE,' said Fump. *'The whole thing was frightening.'*

'I didn't do it on purpose,' said Ray, feeling VERY cross now. 'Also, you were about to zap Droplett in the BOTTOM!'

The word BOTTOM echoed through the long corridor.

To Ray's horror, the deputy head teacher, Miss Myst, was standing right behind her, arms folded and looking very unimpressed.

'Is there a problem with your *bottom*, Miss Grey?' said Miss Myst sternly.

The sniggers from the other students were soon stopped with an icy glare from the severe-looking woman. Her rain cape billowed gently. The glasses perched on her nose were so incredibly tiny, Ray wondered if Miss Myst might need glasses to see her own glasses.

Ray realised the teacher was waiting for an answer.

'No, miss, sorry, miss . . .' Ray mumbled. There was no point in arguing. She HAD shouted when she shouldn't have, and she was feeling far too cross to explain.

'Good,' said the teacher. 'Another outburst like that and you'll be writing a ONE-THOUSAND-word essay in detention about what's wrong with your bottom.'

There was a snort from Frazzle and Fump.

'And don't think you won't be joining her,' the teacher snapped at the twins as she swept her cape to one side and ushered the students in to the Sky Dome.

Miss Myst had only been at Sky Academy for six months as deputy head, and had made it QUITE clear that she neither liked Ray nor approved of her magic. Sure, Ray had once made the whole lunch hall rainbow coloured by mistake, and accidentally taken control of a whole class of snow students and frozen everyone's bottoms to their chairs, but she really was trying her very best.

She didn't mind

studying with La Blaze at the Rainburrow every afternoon while the other students practised their own weather magic together – but deep down, Ray felt more left out at school now than she did when she had no magic at all. She hoped that maybe, one day, the teachers might start to teach rainbow weather magic at school. Maybe then Ray would feel more a part of things.

Ray sat next to Droplett with the other first years in the front row of the Sky Dome. The dome was a large glass structure at the very top of the school, poking out of the treetops with a view of the City of Celestia beyond the forest. The Sky Academy emblem, a huge weathervane, glimmered in the light of the Sunflower.

Ray looked at the empty seat beside her where Snowden usually sat. It was strange not having him at school. Ray hoped he was having fun at the Annual Greatest Snowman Gathering.

But the seat wasn't empty for long, as Percy Wonderwhoosh soon plonked himself down.

'Good morning, Sky Academy!' Miss Myst called out.

'Goooood moooooorning, Miiiiissssss Myyyyyyyyst,' the students droned.

'As you're probably aware,' said Miss Myst, 'I'm standing in as head teacher today, as Professor Glacielle is away with all the other Snow Weatherlings for the Annual Greatest Snowman Gathering.'

'Not ALL,' grumbled Frosty McFlake, the only Snow Weatherling left in school. He didn't turn eleven until the next day, just missing his opportunity to visit the Greatest Snowman.

'I know you're all a little over-excited regarding the recent news about the empty puff pod patch,' continued the deputy head, 'but I urge you all to carry on as normal. Those Cloud Weatherlings with young relatives affected by the empty pods, our thoughts are with you.

Remember, the Council of Forecasters and many others are on the case, so please do NOT let the news affect your schoolwork.'

Ray hugged Nim tightly.

'A reminder that Weather Wobbler practice is at lunchtime,' Miss Myst continued. 'Congratulations to the new team captains, Droplett Dewbells and Alto Wisp.'

Ray nudged Droplett in excitement. She was so proud of her friend! Being captain of the Weather Wobblers team was seriously cool.

Alto stood up and flicked his incredibly shiny white hair, then twirled his cloud-crook. His cloud-dolphin performed a fancy somersault in the air before swimming elegantly around the room. The students erupted with claps and cheers.

'Show-off,' muttered Droplett. She stood up next and swished her cape as hard as she could, absolutely soaking the entire dome of students, before bellowing, 'HONOURED.'

'Thank you for *that*, Miss Dewbells,' said

Miss Myst coldly. 'Moving on. Wind Chime group! You're with Madame Swoosh for an hour this morning. The annual Dingaling Duel is approaching, and Sky Academy hasn't lost in over ten years. We're counting on YOU, Margarie Morningsong!'

A curly-haired second year nodded enthusiastically.

'The rest of you will be heading to your usual morning of General Weather Studies,' continued Miss Myst. 'First years are in for TREAT today with a double dose of good old-fashioned Thermomoteering with Mr Current.'

There was a groan from the front two rows. Ray missed the whoop of joy that would have come from Snowden. He loved the most boring lessons.

'Sky Academy . . . DISMISSED!' sang Miss Myst.

Nim exploded with a **POOF**.

CHAPTER 8
THE SUMMER OF '69

The friends had almost reached the Temperature classrooms in the lower branches of Sky Academy, when they heard a loud wailing sound coming from a second-year classroom further along the corridor.

'What above EARTH is that?' said Droplett.

The friends stood on tiptoes to get a good peek through the second-year classroom window. They saw a girl swinging her cloud-crook around in a frenzy, tears pouring down her face. Sitting next to her was Agent Nephia, scribbling notes in a very concerned manner. Her cloud-slug, Mr Steve, was sitting on the table next to her, looking uninterested. The teacher, a Wind Weatherling called Miss Wheeze, was desperately trying to calm the student down.

'Yikes!' said Droplett. 'I wonder what happened?'

But Ray didn't answer. Something was glowing on the classroom door. It was the same swirly eye symbol she'd seen on the tree trunk next to the puff pod patch the day before.

'There's that eye scrawl again,' said Ray. 'Look!'

'Where? Is it REALLY tiny?' asked Droplett, her nose practically touching the door now.

Ray frowned. 'You honestly can't see it?'

'I WANT MY CLOUD-FLAMINGO?!' the girl bellowed, making Ray and Droplett jump. They peered through the classroom door again and saw Agent Nephia shaking her head.

'Oh no. Another cloud-creature has gone missing,' whispered Ray. She wished she could give Nim a big cuddle, but he still hadn't reappeared. She really hoped he'd turn up soon. The thought of losing him was unbearable!

Ray and Droplett quickly pressed their ears against the door to listen – just as it opened.

They tumbled head first into the classroom.

'Are you two lurking out there for a reason?' Miss Wheeze snapped.

'We heard the crying and wondered if everything was OK?' Ray said as the student's wails grew louder.

'It's none of your business. Get back to your lesson now!' the teacher hissed. 'Otherwise I'll report you both to Miss Myst.'

Ray took Droplett's hand before scooting away, leaving the loud moans behind them – along with the strange glowing eye.

Nim finally reappeared during Ray's Thermomoteering lesson.

'You all right, Nimothy?' asked Ray.

The usually jolly cloud-cat looked a little the worse for wear. He purred once and floated under the table.

'What's got into him?' asked Droplett.

Ray shrugged. 'It took him a long time to reappear, so maybe he's a bit tired,' she said.

'Or hungry.'

'Or bored,' said Droplett. 'We ARE in Thermomoteering, after all.'

Ray and Droplett sat together inside a glass pyramid. The rest of the class were also split into pairs, each sitting in their own temperature-proof pyramids. Having arrived late, Ray had hoped to avoid Mr Current's monotonous introduction. But somehow, he was still talking.

'Every Forecaster owns a thermostat,' he was

droning. 'Before creating the desired weather, they must adjust the temperature accordingly. Whether they're working in a small town, or a large city, the temperature must be JUST right. I once knew a Forecaster who set his thermostat too low, creating a light frost during the summer of '69.' He looked into the middle distance. 'Those were the days. Me and some guys from school had a band. But then Jimmy quit, Jody got married . . .'

Uh-oh, thought Ray. Mr Current was doing it again. Every lesson, he ended up talking about his past. Luckily, he drifted off into his own thoughts pretty swiftly, and the students were free to practise setting their thermostats to the different temperatures.

'I wonder if that missing cloud-flamingo was found,' whispered Droplett, turning the thermometer to zero.

'I h-h-hope so,' said Ray. Her teeth started chattering as their pyramid began to freeze. There was a loud knock on the classroom door.

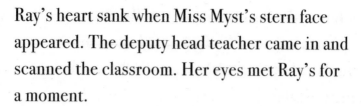

Ray's heart sank when Miss Myst's stern face appeared. The deputy head teacher came in and scanned the classroom. Her eyes met Ray's for a moment.

'A second year's cloud-creature has gone missing,' she said. 'Agent Nephia Weatherwart is on the case and will be questioning all students throughout the day. Hopefully this has nothing to do with the use of *unreliable* magic . . .' she added darkly.

Every student in the class turned to stare at Ray before whispering to each other. Ray felt a bead of sweat trickle down her temple – although that could have been because Droplett was now twiddling her thermostat dial into triple figures. But despite the heat, Ray felt a shiver run down her spine, and a deep sense of unease.

As the Sky Academy wind chime jingled to mark the beginning of lunch, Ray was ready for a change of scenery. She and Droplett headed towards the Weather Wobbler arena in the west of the Forest for a practice session.

'Don't let Miss Myst get you down,' said Droplett, holding Ray's hand. 'She's just being a big fog face.'

'Something's not right, Droplett,' Ray said thoughtfully.

'What do you mean?'

'Something doesn't FEEL right,' Ray said. 'First the baby clouds are missing from the puff pods, and now a fully grown cloud-creature has disappeared. I can't help feeling something odd is going on.' Her tummy rumbled loudly. 'OR I could just be hungry.'

'Well, I say we focus on something happy, like my first practice game as Weather Wobbler team CAPTAIN,' said Droplett with a swish of her cape.

Ray smiled. 'Of course! Sorry, I've been so absorbed with the cloud mystery, when I should be cheering YOU on!' She linked arms with her friend and pulled out a bag of rain-roasted nuts. 'We can eat lunch while we fly over to the Weather Wobbler arena on Nim.'

'Excellent idea!' said Droplett.

Instead of expanding ready for flight, Nim started to shrink.

'Um, Nim, we might need you to make yourself a bit bigger than that so we can fly on you,' Ray said to her cloud-cat.

Nim kept on shrinking.

'Nim? What's wrong?' asked Ray.

But all Nim did was purr sadly and hide behind Ray's ear.

'I don't think he's feeling very well,' Ray said, feeling a pang of worry. 'Sorry, Droplett. We won't be able to fly.'

'Poor Nim,' said Droplett. She gently lifted up her cape. 'I do know an even FASTER way to get to the Weather Wobbler arena, but you might not like it.'

'I don't think we have much choice,' said Ray with a grimace. 'If we walk, we'll be late.'

'Maybe eat your lunch AFTER the puddle-port then,' Droplett suggested.

CHAPTER 9

ALTO WISP

Seconds later the friends had puddle-ported to the main Weather Wobbler arena. It was a huge maze consisting of multiple levels, filled with higgledy-piggledy obstacles.

Droplett jumped up and down with excitement. 'I still can't believe I'm a Weather Wobbler TEAM CAPTAIN!' she sang.

'It doesn't surprise me,' said Ray. 'You're a puddle-porting pro! You make it look SO easy too.'

'Well, Ray, let me tell you – the secret to great puddle-porting is POISE and relaxation. Let the puddle take you . . .' Droplett disappeared into a puddle at her feet, then reappeared again with one great big SPLASH of water.

'I'd not even taken one bite . . .' said a familiar,

slightly grumpy voice.

'Snowden?!' said Ray and Droplett in unison.

There Snowden was, soaking wet, clutching a sandwich and wearing a flamboyant hat.

'Why are you here?' asked Ray.

'And what are you WEARING?' Droplett added.

'I came to watch my best friend play as her first time as Weather Wobbler team captain,' Snowden said with a wonky smile. He peered at his soggy sandwich. 'Although I'm beginning to regret the decision. Oh, and this is the hat that Granny Everfreeze made me to give to the Greatest Snowman. I think it makes me look rather fabulous, don't you?'

'Firstly, I'm not gonna answer that,' said Droplett. 'Secondly, shouldn't that hat be WITH the Greatest Snowman, where you're meant to be with all the other Snow Weatherlings, right now? Don't tell me you missed school too much.'

Snowden sighed. 'Well, you're not wrong. I did miss school. But I'd never have missed the Annual Greatest Snowman Gathering. However . . .'

He half laughed,
half frowned. 'The Greatest
Snowman isn't there any more.'

'What?' said Ray. She
scratched her head. 'The
snowman that has been standing
for over a thousand years is suddenly
gone?'

Still nuzzled behind her ear, Nim miaowed
softly.

'Did it just walk off?' asked Droplett. She
winked and nudged Snowden in the ribs. 'Maybe
it knew YOU were coming!'

'Very funny,' Snowden replied sarcastically.
'Nobody has the foggiest where it went. We think
it finally melted. I'm kind of sad I never got to see
it. So, I figured I'd come back to school. Did
I miss anything good?'

'Ray can update you on today's events while
I prepare for the BEST part of your day,' said
Droplett with a salute. 'The part where I wobble
the weathers out of the other team. I know it's just

a practice game, but I'm still determined to WIN!'

'Good luck, Droplett,' said Ray. 'We'll be cheering you on!'

As Droplett puddle-ported out of sight, Ray took a deep breath and looked at Snowden. 'Let's grab a good seat and I'll fill you in . . .' she said.

'Sizzling snowflakes!' said Snowden, after Ray had told him about the day's events.

'Something strange is going on,' said Ray, bracing her staff. 'And I'm going to get to the bottom of it.'

Nim mewed sadly in her ear.

'Not to mention,' Ray added, 'something isn't right with poor Nim.'

The solemn cloud-cat floated into Ray's lap before returning to normal cat size.

'Could be a case of Under-the-Weather syndrome?' Snowden suggested. 'I hear it's going around.'

There was a huge spark followed by a RUMBLE from the Thunder 'n' Lightning commentators, marking the beginning of the Weather Wobbler practice game.

'There's Droplett!' said Ray, happily waving at their friend. 'I really hope her team wins.'

'They'll win,' Snowden replied simply. 'Have you seen the captain of the opposing team? He's too busy showing off.'

It was true. Alto Wisp was twisting his cloud-crook around before striking another pose with a pout. His cloud-dolphin was balancing on her tail fins next to him, spinning slowly on the spot.

There was another crackle of lightning, followed by a grumble of thunder.

'Welcome to the first practice game of the season!' said the commentators together. 'It is the job of the team captain to move the chosen object through the maze using only weather magic. The first one to get the object into the windsock goal at the end of the Wobstacle course WINS. If you touch the object, you are disqualified. If the object is dropped, you will have to start the whole maze again. As you know, for every game we have a brand-new random object donated by a fellow citizen for each team. Today, for Droplett Dewbells' team, we have a rather luxurious hat, courtesy of a *mystery* Weatherling!'

Snowden squinted and patted his head. 'That's MY hat! Droplett must have stolen it when she puddle-ported away. Honestly!'

Ray couldn't help chuckling as the team players filtered into the arena.

'And Alto Wisp's team will be moving an egg, donated by Ray Grey's father,' said the thunder commentator with a small rumble of cheers. 'Thanks, Haze Grey!'

'OK, Weather Wobblers,' said the lightning commentator. 'Good luck and MAKE THE SKY WOBBLE!'

Lightning crackled to mark the start of the race. There was a cheer and claps from the few supportive students who had come along to the arena to watch their friends' practice game. Droplett and Alto set off at full speed through the Wobstacle course. Droplett kept the luxurious hat afloat using her rain magic, while Alto Wisp was hot on her heels, riding on the back of his cloud-dolphin at top speed with the egg balanced on the cloud-creature's head.

Droplett puddle-ported to dodge wobstacles created by the opposing team as they attempted to WOBBLE the hat out of her rainy grasp with zaps of lightning or huge wafts of wind. She was FAST – but somehow Alto was FASTER. He sailed through the air with such poise it was hard not to be impressed.

'Uh-oh! Alto's team are winning,' said Ray, hoping Droplett could catch up.

A fourth-year Wind Weatherling called Fluster Force blew into his wind-flute, sending Droplett and the hat swirling along the Wobstacle course, where it narrowly avoided a giant snow-spider's icy web.

'COME ON, DROPLETT!' Ray shouted.

'Don't let them wobble you!'

Droplett swished her cape, conjuring a puddle in front of a wall of lightning. She and the hat disappeared into the puddle, reappearing on the other side of the lightning wall safe and sound. They were back in the game!

But Alto Wisp was already approaching the windsock goal at the end of the course. He guided his cloud-dolphin through the maze as she juggled the egg perfectly between her floofy flippers.

But then something strange started to happen.

'What above Earth . . .?' Ray muttered. 'Alto's cloud-dolphin is disappearing.'

Alto Wisp was desperately waving his cloud-crook around in an attempt to bring his cloud-dolphin back. But it was no good. Moments later, the cloud-dolphin had completely GONE, and down Alto fell – along with the very old egg.

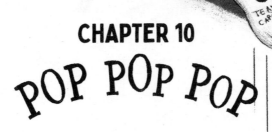

CHAPTER 10

POP POP POP

Ray needed to do something FAST. She whipped out her rainbow staff and pointed it in the direction of Alto as he fell. She couldn't afford to make a mistake, so Ray decided to stick with one rainbow gift she knew REALLY well. Rainbow Slide's gift!

Ray pulled her staff back over her head, then forward again, as if making a large paint stroke across the sky. She felt her magic pulse through her as a large rainbow poured out from the tip of the staff and through the air towards the flailing boy.

Alto went skimming along the band of colours all the way to the ground, landing safely and softly.

Ray lowered her staff and the large rainbow

slide faded away. She ran down to the pitch as fast as she could with Snowden and Nim, as the other team players rushed over to a shell-shocked Alto. Given the really yucky smell in the air, there was absolutely NO doubt that the old egg had been broken in the fall.

'Alto! Are you OK?!' Ray asked breathlessly.

'He's in one piece, thanks to you, Ray,' said Droplett. She knelt down next to the Cloud Weatherling and rubbed his shoulder.

Alto was scratching his head and looking very confused. 'Where's Penelope?' he croaked. 'Is she all right? Penelope?!' He lifted his cloud-crook and moved it in a circular motion. But nothing happened. 'My cloud magic!' he said. 'I . . . I can't use it!'

'Can you remember what happened?' asked Ray. 'Just before Penelope disappeared?'

But Alto wasn't listening. He was looking around desperately for his cloud-companion.

'Try not to panic,' said Snowden. 'Penelope has to be here somewhere.'

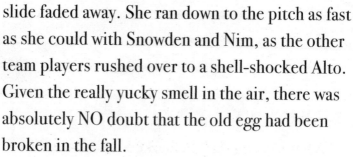

The Sky Academy gameskeeper Mr Windle marched across the grounds, the large wind-trombone strapped to his back shimmering in the Sunflower's light. He was a force of nature, and not to be messed with.

'What's going on?' he barked. 'Alto – you almost won! Where's Penelope?'

'That's the thing, sir,' said the cloud boy. 'I don't know. She just disappeared.'

Alto locked eyes with Ray. He pointed at her.

'Y-you must have done something,' he cried. 'I saw the *Weekly Weathervane* this morning. You did something to the puff pods too!'

'Oi! Ray just SAVED your life,' said Droplett.

'She did something to Penelope!' Alto said, louder now.

'Yeah, she used her weird rainbow magic,' said another student from Alto's team. 'She wanted us to LOSE the game.'

Mr Windle shot Ray a disapproving look. 'You used weather magic to tamper with the game?' he asked.

103

'No!' Ray protested. 'I mean, yes, I used magic, but not to tamper with the game. I was saving Alto. He was about to face the same fate as that egg!'

She nodded at the stinky mess a few metres away. Then something else caught her eye. Snowden's hat lay on the ground beside the splattered egg. Something glowed gently on the rim. A familiar-looking shape.

Ray ran over and picked the hat up. 'The eye symbol again,' she said with a gasp.

'What's going on?' asked Droplett, joining Ray.

'It's the eye I keep seeing,' said Ray. 'Just like the eye I saw on the tree trunk by the puff pods AND on the second-year classroom door . . .'

Droplett frowned. 'I still can't see what you're talking about.'

'I don't understand,' Ray cried. 'Why can't you see it?'

'RAY GREY,' boomed Mr Windle. 'How dare you run off while I'm talking to you!'

'Sorry, sir. I just noticed a strange eye on
the hat. I keep seeing it everywhere,' said Ray,
pointing to the rim. 'Look! It's glowing. I thought
it might be a Sky Scrawler, but I don't know . . .
I feel like it might be something more.'

The other students scoffed and laughed.
But Ray didn't notice. Her mind was racing.

'Every time cloud-creatures have gone

missing, I've seen the eye,' she muttered. 'What if they're connected?'

The teacher looked at Ray as if she were speaking backwards before snatching the hat from her grip. He held it up to the other students.

'Does anyone else SEE a glowing EYE on this hat?'

The students shook their heads. Ray didn't understand. It was RIGHT THERE in front of them, glowing as bright as anything!

'You!' the teacher barked, pointing at Snowden. 'Do YOU see this eye?'

Snowden gulped. 'I . . . I . . . think if I squint a lot, I might . . .' he stammered. Three big think-flakes popped out from his right ear. POP POP POP. Ray knew that meant Snowden was lying, but she appreciated his efforts to cover up for her.

'I think that's the practice game over for today, kids,' said Mr Windle. He scribbled on a piece of paper, screwed it up into a ball and threw it into the air. Then he blew into his trombone, sending the note zipping in the direction of the school.

Five minutes later, a puddle emerged, and Miss Myst appeared. Ray's heart sank. Nim hissed at the teacher, then exploded.

Seconds later, a familiar-looking cloud-slug lumbered into the arena with Agent Nephia on its back. The cloud detective guided Mr Steve to the ground with her cloud-crook and tipped her hat at the assembled crowd.

'I overheard the news,' she sang, pulling out her pom-pom-topped pen. 'Do not fear, darlings. I am on the CASE!'

'Agent Nephia!' said Ray in relief. At least SHE might believe Ray.

'Mr Windle, this is Agent Nephia, head of the Bureau of Unexplained Meteorological Sightings,' said Miss Myst.

'B.U.M.S. for short,' said Agent Nephia cheerfully.

'She's been investigating the empty puff pods and the recent disappearance of a cloud-flamingo,' said Miss Myst. 'Your wind-note claimed another cloud-creature has disappeared?'

'Alto's cloud-dolphin Penelope disappeared during the practice game,' said Mr Windle.

'That IS curious,' said Nephia, scribbling in her notebook.

'Ray did it,' Alto sniffed. 'She used her magic on me.'

'I didn't! I was just trying to save you!' Ray said. She turned to Agent Nephia. 'He was falling so I tried to help.'

'She's telling the truth,' said Snowden. 'I was next to Ray the whole time.'

'Ray seems to think there's some kind of glowing eye on this weird hat too,' said Mr Windle, giving the hat to Miss Myst.

'Um, that's my hat,' Snowden added, raising a hand. 'And it's not weird. Granny Everfreeze calls it *Au Peculiaire*.'

Miss Myst studied the hat and frowned. All the

while, Agent Nephia was furiously scribbling away with Mr Steve floating next to her.

'I don't know what she did,' Alto said, 'but I can't use my magic. I feel . . . empty.'

'Miss Myst, please,' pleaded Ray. 'Something strange is happening. I can draw the eye for you. I keep seeing it where the cloud-creatures are disappearing.'

'The only strange thing here is your magic,' muttered Miss Myst.

Ray flinched. She noticed Agent Nephia shoot Miss Myst a dark glance too.

'I heard you were also lurking outside the classroom when the second-year's cloud-flamingo went missing,' said the deputy head. 'You say that this EYE is in all the places the cloud-creatures have disappeared. But it appears that YOU are also in all of those places, Ray Grey.'

Ray's cheeks were on fire. She hated that Miss Myst was right. 'I *was* in those places, but honestly, I didn't make any of those cloud-creatures disappear!'

But Miss Myst narrowed her eyes and raised her chin. Then, with an air of superiority, she said, 'Tell that to your parents, Miss Grey. *You* are hereby expelled from Sky Academy.'

CHAPTER 11
A SECRET SHELF!

EXPELLED . . . The word spiralled around Ray's head like a sickening whirlwind.

Even Agent Nephia looked shocked. 'Dribbling drizzlepops!' she cried.

'You can't expel Ray!' cried Droplett.

'Miss Dewbells, I don't think you're in a position to be arguing with the *acting head* right now,' said Miss Myst. 'I hear you've been teetering on the edge of expulsion since the day you started at Sky Academy.' Droplett opened her mouth to speak, but the teacher put up a hand. 'One more word and you'll join Ray.'

Droplett growled.

Ray squeezed her friend's hand gently. 'Don't get into trouble for me,' she whispered.

'Everyone back to Sky Academy now!' commanded Miss Myst. 'Including you, Miss Grey. I'll call your parents.'

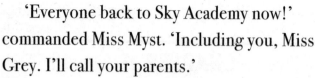

Ray was sent to the Lower Sky library for the remainder of lunchtime. She felt really glum.

'I was just trying to help,' she muttered.

Nim had finally reformed from his explosion in a VERY glum state himself. He mewed gently and laid his head on Ray's arm while she scribbled absent-mindedly on the back of the expulsion letter her parents had to sign.

Ray had never dreamed in a windillion years that SHE would ever get expelled. She hadn't gone to Lower Weather School like her friends when she was younger because she had no magic. Instead, she had visited lots of libraries and museums. That was when she discovered La Blaze DeLight's books. And THAT was when Ray had decided she wanted to be an Earth Explorer.

Ray was SO excited when she found out that she'd be going to the Upper Weather School,

Sky Academy. Sky Academy taught subjects such as General Weather Studies, Earth Studies and Weather History every morning, which didn't require any magic practice. Even though it always took Ray a little longer to read, she loved the challenges and the problem solving, no matter how tricky. And she loved spending every day with her BEST friends.

Now she *finally* had weather magic, and her second year at school would have been full of even MORE exciting subjects and school trips. But Ray wouldn't get to do any of that now.

'Hey, Ray,' said a friendly voice. Gusty Gavin the librarian pulled up a chair at the tree-stump desk in the corner of the library. 'I heard what happened.'

Ray kept scribbling to keep herself calm. 'Things were easier when I had no magic at all,' she said sadly. 'I don't mind so much if others are a bit weirded out by me. The part that bothers me the most is the fact they don't *trust* me. I just try to help, but it only makes things worse.'

'Some people are scared of what they don't understand,' Gusty Gavin said softly.

'But I'm not scary,' said Ray, looking up at Gavin.

The librarian chortled. 'Not at all. But the Weatherlands haven't seen rainbow weather magic in over a thousand years. And you've got the power of not just ONE Rainbow Weatherling, but a whole clan! Everyone needs to be patient while you learn your new skills.'

'I can already make a pretty good rainbow slide,' said Ray shyly.

'Well, there you go!' said Gusty Gavin. 'And without that slide, Alto Wisp would've been as flat as a pitter patter pancake.'

He winked – but then his expression changed and his face turned pale. 'W-what are you drawing there?' he said, and pointed shakily towards the letter Ray had been scribbling on.

Ray looked down. 'This?' she said, staring at her swirly eye doodles. 'I keep seeing this glowing eye everywhere, I thi–'

'You have to rip that up!' Gusty Gavin
interrupted in an urgent whisper. He looked
terrified.

Ray was taken aback. 'But I have to give it to
my parents,' she said, feeling very confused.

The librarian shook his head. He tapped the
doodles. 'You can't have anyone see that.'

'But they're just drawings of eyes,' said Ray.

Gusty Gavin got to his feet. He checked around
for other students once more before saying under
his breath, 'Follow me.'

Ray trotted behind Gusty Gavin as he weaved through the many book-filled tree branches that made up the library until they reached a particularly thick and grimy looking branch. There were no books here, and it was covered in some kind of black speckled mould.

Gavin held a finger up to his lips, prompting Ray to stay quiet. Taking hold of his wind-bugle he blew into it gently, one long blast followed by three short toots. To Ray's amazement the black mould disappeared, and the branch became hollow. Inside was a row of thick books.

'A secret shelf!' Ray gasped.

Gavin shot her a warning glance. 'You must not tell anyone about this. These are NOT to be read by students. Do you promise?'

'I double triple rainbow promise,' said Ray with a salute, leaning forward to get a better look at the spines of the books.

Gavin pulled out a book with *The Book of Forbidden Forces* printed on the spine. 'This book is full of forbidden weather spells,' he said.

'If any of these spells are used, a Weatherling is sent STRAIGHT to Precipitory Prison without so much as a Temperature Trial.'

Ray gulped. 'Wobbling weathervanes. So why is a book like that in a school?'

'Because it's the last place you'd expect it,' said Gusty Gavin. 'I'm the keeper of the books, good or bad, and I've been trusted to guard these and make sure they don't get into the wrong hands. They require a LOT of power.'

He flicked through the pages, then stopped and passed the book to Ray. The swirly illustration of an eye sat in the centre of the open page. Above were written the words:

EYE OF THE STORM.

CHAPTER 12

THAT WON'T BE NECESSARY

Ray studied the text carefully, but the writing was so curly and tiny and the letters got terribly jumbled. Nim pawed at the page and miaowed desperately.

'Ray, did you say you *saw* this eye?' asked Gavin.

'MISS GREY?!' came a voice from somewhere in the library.

Nim exploded. Gavin stared at Ray with wide, panicked eyes. Without thinking, Ray stuffed the book into her bag. Gusty Gavin used his wind magic to seal the secret branch shelf back up. The mould reappeared and it just looked like an old, grubby empty shelf once more.

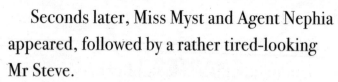

Seconds later, Miss Myst and Agent Nephia
appeared, followed by a rather tired-looking
Mr Steve.

'We can't get hold of your parents, so Agent
Nephia will take you to your next of kin, Aunt
Foggaleena,' said the deputy head sternly.
'Now, where's your expulsion letter?'

'Oh, Nim ate it before he exploded,' lied Ray,
scrumpling up the paper and tucking it into her
pocket. 'We can wait for him to poop it out if
you like?'

Miss Myst wrinkled her nose. 'That won't be
necessary. We shall write another. Come along.'

Ray looked desperately at Gavin, who
was giving her a YOU-STILL-HAVE-A-
FORBIDDEN-BOOK-IN-YOUR-BAG kind of
look. She couldn't very well stop to say, *'Oh, hey
Miss Myst, don't mind me while I put this highly
dangerous book back in the secret shelf I shouldn't
know about.'* So, for now, the book was heading
home with Ray.

Nim hadn't reformed yet, so Agent Nephia

serenaded Ray on the back of Mr Steve the cloud-slug, all the way to Aunt Foggaleena's house in the Windvane Village. So far, Ray had heard operatic versions of 'Wind Beneath My Knickers' and 'Here Comes the Moon'.

'Darling, I'm so sorry you got expelled,' said Agent Nephia, guiding the lolloping slug with her curly cloud-crook through the skies. 'I shouldn't really say this, but your deputy head teacher is a bit of a fog goblin.'

Ray found herself smiling. 'She's had it in for me from day one,' she admitted. 'I bet she's been hoping for a reason to expel me.'

'Want to know a secret?' asked Agent Nephia. 'I was expelled a long time ago.'

'Really?' asked Ray. 'What did you do?'

Agent Nephia looked genuinely upset. 'I was just trying to help a friend.'

'Exactly like me!' said Ray.

Agent Nephia gave a wistful smile. 'It must be quite lonely being the only Rainbow Weatherling?' she asked.

Ray sighed. 'It is a bit,' she said. 'I never had any magic before . . . but somehow now I DO have some, it's even trickier.'

'Perhaps being at home isn't so bad,' said Agent Nephia. 'It means you can focus on your rainbow weather magic studies. Find out about all those special rainbow gifts stored up inside of you, eh? How lovely to have so much intriguing magic to learn.'

Ray sat up a little straighter. 'You're right,'

she said with determination. 'I'm going to prove that my magic can help find those baby clouds. There must be at least ONE rainbow gift inside me that can help.' She fist-pumped the air and almost slipped off the cloud-slug.

With a chuckle, Agent Nephia held her cloud-crook out to stop Ray from falling off. 'What rainbow gifts have you learned so far?' she asked.

It was so nice for Ray to talk to someone who was genuinely interested in her magic! 'I've nailed

Rainbow Slide's gift,' she said, counting them off on her fingers. 'I tried Rainbow Retrieve's, but accidently summoned a baby fog goblin. The one I REALLY want to learn is Rainbow Beard's gift.'

Agent Nephia burst out laughing. 'What above Earth does that gift do?!'

'I've no idea yet,' said Ray with a shrug. 'Me and my friends have been looking through ALL of Rainbow Beard's notes, but there's nothing about HIS unique gift anywhere.'

'I'd leave that one out. There are far more important rainbow gifts you should be focusing on.' Agent Nephia sounded more serious now. 'Especially if you want to prove you're not responsible for the missing clouds.'

The cloud detective guided Mr Steve down to the Windvane Village, skidding to a halt outside Aunt Foggaleena's house.

'Thank you for the ride,' said Ray as she swung herself off the cloud-slug.

Agent Nephia elegantly twirled her cloud-crook around in her fingers like a baton and saluted with the other hand. 'Remember, you have my card if you need me,' she said. And she tipped her large hat before taking to the skies once again on Mr Steve, singing a song about curly raindrops.

There was a small, squeaking sound behind Ray. A teeny-tiny but familiar floofy cloud-cat was forming in the air, but without a head.

'Nim, you're back!' said Ray. 'There's my favourite cloud.'

Nim's head finally appeared. He miaowed sadly and then flattened out, resembling a floofy rug with teeny dot eyes.

'Oh, Nimothy, what's wrong?' Ray stroked his flat face gently. 'I guess you must be feeling scared from hearing about all the cloud-creatures disappearing. But don't worry, I'm going to find out what's going on . . .' She stood up tall and put her hands on her hips. 'Because I AM RAINBOW GREY!'

Her voice echoed through the village. There was a shuffle in the house behind her, then a *creeeeak* as the door opened.

'I should have known it was *you*,' Aunt Foggaleena grumbled. 'Expelled, eh? Typical!'

Ray's arms dropped by her sides. 'Hi, Aunty,' she mumbled. 'I just need to stay here until Mum and Dad are back home, if that's OK?'

'No, it's not OK,' said her aunt. 'I told your teacher you are not welcome here after scaring my children at the puff pod party yesterday AND destroying my darling Cloudiculus's hopes of ever having a cloud-companion. You can wait outside.'

Without another word, Aunt Foggaleena slammed the door shut.

Ray stood for a moment in shock.

'Well, that was rude,' she said at last. 'Come on, Nim. I know one place we'll definitely still be welcome.'

CHAPTER 13

THE LEAST WORST PART

'Raaaaaay!' sang La Blaze as Ray slid into the Rainburrow a few minutes later. 'I have GOOD NEWS!'

Ray twiddled her blue streak of hair. 'I have not-so-good news,' she replied.

La Blaze looked sympathetic. 'Wanna go first?'

Ray plonked herself down between two huge piles of rainbow weather magic notes. 'Actually, why don't you go first?' She pulled out her screwed-up expulsion letter and gripped her bag where the VERY BAD book was hidden.

'Well,' said La Blaze, settling herself on to the edge of the tree stump in the centre of the burrow. 'I was reading through this HUGE book on

rainbow weather magic lore.' She flicked through the many pages. 'Oh yes, I found out this little fact too – did you know you that can't take control of another fellow Rainbow Weatherling's power?'

Ray lifted an eyebrow. 'That IS handy to know, but I guess it doesn't really matter since I'm the only Rainbow Weatherling in existence right now,' she said.

'Ah yes, very true,' said La Blaze, continuing to look through the pages of the huge book. 'Aha! There it is . . . It was in this chapter about rainbow weather magic and the Forest of Fahrenheits . . .'

La Blaze cleared her throat and read:

> *Rainbow weather magic is unable to control*
> *or alter any type of weather that is NOT*
> *connected to a Weatherling. So, for example,*
> *a Rainbow Weatherling CANNOT alter*
> *the flora found in the Forest of Fahrenheits,*
> *including lightning leaves, one-eyed windflits,*
> *puff pods or giggling gollybobs. This is*
> *because the magic is not connected to a*

Weatherling (or in the case of a puff pod, not YET connected to a Weatherling).

'That means I can't have made the baby clouds disappear!' gasped Ray, sitting up straighter. She was so happy she ran over to hug La Blaze, tripping on a tree root on the way and plummeting head first into a box of unerupted rumblebuns.

SPLAT! SPLAT! SPLAT! SPLAT!

'Billowing breezes, are you OK?!' asked La Blaze, helping a syrup-covered Ray to her feet. She giggled. 'Perhaps we can postpone that hug for when you're a little less sticky?'

Nim started to lick the pink goo from Ray's cheeks as La Blaze patted the space next to her. 'Now we've established your magic can't have affected the puff pods, how about you share the not-so-good news?' she said.

'I'll start with the least-worst part,' said Ray. 'I got expelled.'

'That's the LEAST worst part?' shrieked La Blaze. 'But why?'

'I think there might be some really bad magic at work,' said Ray.

La Blaze blinked. 'I've not left this underground base for SIX months,' she said. 'I have literally NO IDEA what's going on up in the Weatherlands or down on Earth. And you've just informed me that you've been expelled, and there's really bad magic at work? Please forgive me if I'm a *little* confused.'

Ray updated La Blaze on Agent Nephia, the strange eye symbol, the missing cloud-creatures and the Weather Wobbler game that went wrong. When she finished, the Sun Weatherling let out a long whistle.

'Well,' she said. 'I think YOU win on the most eventful life right now.'

'And the most sticky!' said Ray, desperately trying to remove a big dollop of rumblebun syrup from her shoe. She finally dislodged the goo, but accidently kicked her school bag at the same time – and *The Book of Forbidden Forces* went skidding across the room.

La Blaze stared at the book.

'I can explain . . .' Ray started.

But La Blaze covered her eyes with her hands. 'I NEVER SAW THAT BOOK,' she gasped. 'Ray . . . why have you got that BAD book?'

'Please don't tell anyone I've got it! I didn't mean to keep it,' said Ray, picking it up. 'Gusty Gavin showed it to me. I think it has information about the glowing eye symbol I keep seeing everywhere –'

'STOP!' snapped La Blaze as Ray went to open the book.

Ray had never seen La Blaze look so worried. She slowly slid the book back into her bag.

'I'm sorry,' said La Blaze more gently. 'That book should NOT be out in the open. The spells in that book are forbidden for a reason. They are too powerful. In the wrong hands they can put the Earth and skies in deep danger.'

'But what if the eye I'm seeing is connected to the empty puff pods and the disappearing cloud-creatures?' asked Ray. 'I might be able to figure out a way to stop it. I can help!'

But La Blaze shook her head. 'Ray, you can't do anything to stop a Forbidden Spell. You need to return that book to wherever you found it. Do NOT tamper with that kind of magic. Promise me you'll take it back to where you got it from?'

Ray sighed. 'OK.'

Luckily La Blaze didn't spot the crossed fingers behind her back.

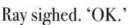

It was time to practise her magic. Ray flicked through the list of ancient Weatherlings. She still

couldn't believe she was now the owner of ALL their rainbow gifts.

'So, what have you learned so far?' asked La Blaze checking off a long list of rainbow gifts stuck to the root-covered walls.

'Well, I think I'll need to practise the retrieving lost weather gift so I don't end up finding unwanted things . . . Shrinking the weather was easy until the cloud-creatures exploded, then I THOUGHT rewinding the weather would be a breeze, but I ended up making the cloud-creatures explode on repeat. The
only gift I seem to be able to do without making any mistakes is the one where I can make a rainbow slide.'

'Well, let's try a new one today,' La Blaze suggested. 'Then we can recap the others after . . .'

'Actually,' said Ray lowering the papers. 'Can we learn about Rainbow Beard's gift? I really want to know what it can do.' She thought back to Nephia's comment – *I'd leave that one out. There are far more important rainbow gifts you should be focusing on* – but somehow Ray was even MORE intrigued. Surely every gift was useful in its own way? Otherwise what was the point in having one?!

La Blaze grimaced. 'Ray, I've looked windillion and one times for information on Rainbow Beard's gift. But there's literally NOTHING here about it.'

'It makes no sense,' said Ray. 'Rainbow Beard was the professor of a rainbow school. This is HIS old base . . . surely he had information on his own ability?'

La Blaze shrugged. 'Sorry, kid, I'm stumped. Trust me, I've hunted high and low since I've been living down here. Anyway, let's be honest, a gift to do with BEARDS doesn't sound like the most useful gift!'

'Hmmm, that's what Nephia said,' grumbled Ray. 'But what if it is useful? What if it gives me the ability to grow a rainbow beard?! Not only would I look GREAT, it would be an excellent disguise and make me feel ever so grown-up . . . and –'

'OK, OK! I'll have another look for any
information on it,' La Blaze laughed. 'But we're
running out of practice time for today, how about
we learn THIS one . . . ?' She lifted up a picture
of a Rainbow Weatherling with a big round
forcefield surrounding her.

'Rainbow Bubble,' she read out. 'Rainbow
Bubble's gift creates a colourful and impenetrable
forcefield, making it impossible for any other
weather magic to affect them. Weather magic
can pass out from inside the bubble, but weather
magic CANNOT get in from the outside.'

Ray grinned and prodded at the page. 'I want
to learn how to do that!'

If Ray was going to have to dabble with some
forbidden magic and quite possibly ROGUES,
then a protective bubble would come in very
handy. Plus, it just sounded really fun.

La Blaze read out the instructions.

'Stick your staff firmly into the ground.
As the rainbow colours begin to form, gently lift

the staff upwards and hold with both hands, before spinning around in a clockwise direction. After one full turn, place the staff back into the ground. The bubble forcefield should be ready. But you must focus to keep it going.' She looked at Ray. 'Want to try?'

Ray nodded and placed her staff firmly on the root-covered ground. She took a deep breath.

Colours flashed through Ray's mind, then flooded from the top of the staff. *SPIN!* she thought. Ray lifted the staff and spun on the spot, VERY nearly falling over but holding her balance in the nick of time. As she placed the staff back into the ground, there was an almighty POP, making Ray jump – and she found herself inside a HUGE rainbow bubble.

'I DID IT!' she cheered. There was another POP and the bubble was gone. She grimaced. 'Now I just need to learn to keep it going . . .'

It felt like no time had passed before Snowden and Droplett arrived at the Rainburrow. Ray was on

her third round of bubble practice.

'Guys! LOOK! It's a bubble of protection,' Ray cried, creating another bubble around her friends. 'No magic can get IN, but our magic can still get OUT.'

'That's VERY handy!' said Snowden, unwrapping a drizzle-pickle sandwich.

'Let's test it!' said Droplett.

She stepped swiftly out of the bubble
and swished her cloak as hard as she could.
Unfortunately, the stream of rainwater passed
right through the bubble wall as easy as anything,
completely soaking Ray, Snowden and (as usual)
his sandwich.

'I thought you said weather magic couldn't
get IN?!' squeaked Snowden.

'I guess I haven't perfected it yet,' Ray
grimaced, wiping the rainwater from her face.
'Sorry! How was the rest of school?'

'Not the same without you,' Snowden replied sadly.

'We still can't believe you got expelled,' said Droplett. 'If one of us was ever gonna get expelled, I always thought it would be me!'

'But that's not all,' said Snowden. 'More cloud-creatures have gone missing. Tilly Tuft's cloud-platypus, and the fourth-year teacher Mr Flurray's cloud-hedgehog.' He shook his head. 'Miss Myst said that all cloud magic lessons might have to be cancelled if it carries on.'

'Wobbling weathervanes! That's awful,' cried Ray.

'The fact the cloud-creatures are STILL disappearing and you're not even at school PROVES it has nothing to do with you, Ray,' said Snowden. 'I tried to explain that to Miss Myst so she'd let you come back, but you know what she's like. She won't admit that she might be wrong about you.'

'Something really weird is DEFINITELY going on,' Droplett added.

'Thanks for believing in me guys,' said Ray earnestly. 'You're right, I think something –'

'ACHOO!'

Snowden erupted with a nose full of tiny snowballs.

'AAAAAACHOO! ACHOO!'

'What's wrong with you?!' asked Droplett.

Snowden was red-faced and his eyes were watering. A tiny icicle was dangling from his nostril. 'Sorry. I think my allergies are flaring up. It makes no sense. I'm only allergic to stardust and pigeons . . .'

Something small and feathery came hurtling down the rainbow slide into the burrow. Ray pointed her rainbow staff towards the creature. Droplett braced her rain cape and Snowden tried desperately not to sneeze again.

La Blaze ran over to a rather dishevelled-looking pigeon.

'Coo La La?!' she said.

CHAPTER 14

A SUPRISE VISITOR

Coo La La had been a friend of La Blaze, back in her Rogue days. He had left La Blaze's side six months earlier and hadn't been seen since. La Blaze and Ray figured he'd settled somewhere on Earth.

Coo La La's black and white speckled feathers were sticking out every which way, and the pigeon's tiny monocle was cracked.

'Is he . . . dead?' asked Droplett.

She swished her cape gently and splashed the pigeon with cold rainwater. This seemed to help. He took in a large gasp of breath, his eyes wide and full of fear.

'She's . . . she's back!' the pigeon stammered.

Ray and her friends looked at each other.

'Who's back?' asked Ray.

The pigeon gulped. 'Tornadia Twist.'

Ray had NOT expected that answer. She felt as if ice-cold water had been poured all over her too. The WORST Rogue in history? The Rogue who had used Shadow Essence to take away the magic of every Rainbow Weatherling a thousand years ago? Impossible!

La Blaze blew a loud raspberry. 'You disappear for six months, then THIS is how to greet us on your return?!' she said, putting her hands on her hips. She turned to Ray. 'He always had a twisted sense of humour.'

Ray expected the pigeon to retaliate with a witty comeback, but he didn't. He just looked at La Blaze blankly.

La Blaze was clearly taken aback by the pigeon's lack of response. 'Tornadia can't possibly be back!' she spluttered. 'She'd be WELL over a thousand years old by now. Nobody lives that long.' She looked at Snowden. 'Do they?'

'If she HAS lived that long, then she can't be

looking too good,' said Snowden.

'Coo La La must have bumped his head,' said Droplett.

'I DID NOT!' the pigeon shouted.

Ray lowered herself to the ground so she was level with Coo La La. 'Do you think you can tell us what happened?' she asked.

Coo La La blinked a few times, then cleared his throat. 'When I left the Weatherlands six months ago, I arrived on Earth and commandeered the best sandcastle I could find,' he said. 'Then I thought I saw a shooting star, so I was about to make a wish for a TEN TURRET sandcastle. But lightning struck, and my beautiful castle fell into a huge crack in the ground. Then a scary-looking person with swirly black and white hair was standing in front of me –'

'AHA!' La Blaze cut in. 'Tornadia Twist was a *Rainbow* Weatherling. All Rainbow Weatherlings had rainbow-coloured hair like Ray. So it couldn't possibly have been Tornadia.'

'She also had one purple and one blue eye,'

said Coo La La.

'Oh,' said La Blaze.

Ray shivered. Every Rainbow Weatherling, including Ray, was born with one purple and one blue eye. The trait was unique to Rainbow Weatherlings.

'She put me in a bucket with a lid and chucked me into the sea!' cried Coo La La. 'Days passed. I thought I was PIGEON DUST, until some surfers found me and took me to the Bird Rescue Sanctuary. Once I was strong enough, I escaped from their clutches and flew all the way back here.' He took in a deep breath. 'We must tell the Council of Forecasters *now*.'

'But it CAN'T have been Tornadia!' said La Blaze. 'Why would she be back after a thousand years? How could she have survived for so long?'

'Both good points,' said Snowden, his ears practically erupting with think-flakes. 'But there's a more important question. If Tornadia Twist is back, then where is she now?'

Ray gulped.

'What if she's here, in the Weatherlands?' said Droplett.

'If she is, then she's keeping very quiet about it.' Ray's mind was positively swirling. 'Surely someone as powerful and vengeful as Tornadia would have just blasted into the Weatherlands and created a huge storm by now? I don't get it . . .'

'Maybe she likes to plan her villainous return properly?' Snowden suggested. 'Slow and steady wins the race, eh?' He grinned, but nobody returned his smile.

'Perhaps if we know more about Tornadia Twist's rainbow gift, it might help work out if it's really her?' said Ray.

She headed over to the Rainburrow's central tree stump, which was piled high with notes on rainbow weather magic. La Blaze had organised all the Rainbow Weatherlings and their gifts in alphabetical order, with colour-coded tabs. Ray ran her finger through the pages until she got to the letter T, and pulled out the notes on Rainbow Twist. That had been Tornadia's name before she went Rogue.

Nim pawed at the paper and hissed. Ray wondered what Tornadia had been like before deciding to turn on her fellow Rainbow Weatherlings. Had she been NICE once upon a time? Why had she taken all of the other Rainbow Weatherlings' magic?

'Rainbow Twist has the ability to twist one type of weather into another,' Ray read aloud.

Snowden's nostrils streamed with think-flakes.

'That's a pretty powerful gift.'

Nim expanded and miaowed loudly. Ray felt like he was trying to tell her something. She just wished she knew what it was.

A dial on a Compass Caller dangling from the door to the Rainburrow suddenly began to whirl around frantically. Ray ran over and lifted the lid.

'Hello?' she said.

'Ray, is that you?' came the fizzy sound of her mum's voice. 'I need you to come home right now.'

'Sure,' Ray said. 'But Mum, there's something you should kn–'

'Hurry back!' her mum said firmly, and hung up.

'Do you think your mum found out about you getting expelled?' asked Droplett with a grimace.

'Probably,' said Ray, feeling a pang of worry. 'Come on, we'd better go.'

'Good luck,' said La Blaze. 'I'll be here if you need me. I'll look after Coo La La. I think he's in need of some comfort.'

There was a flurry of feathers before the pigeon flew up the rainbow slide chute and disappeared.

'Or not,' sighed La Blaze.

Ray, Snowden and Droplett stepped out of the Rainbow Weatherstone.

'Ready for a super speedy flight, Nim?' said Ray.

The cloud-cat hid himself in Ray's school bag.

'Please, Nim!' said Ray feeling a little frustrated. 'Why do you keep doing this?'

Droplett was already holding the edges of her cape, a big puddle at her feet poised for porting.

'Come on then,' she said, beckoning Ray and a very reluctant Snowden over to her. She winked. 'I think I'm gonna have to start charging for all these puddle-taxi-rides!'

As soon as they arrived back at Cloud Nine, Ray's mum ran over, followed by Ray's dad.

'Mum, Dad – I can explain about being exp–' began Ray, thinking she was about to get a massive telling off.

But Cloudia and Haze didn't look angry. In fact, they looked incredibly sad.

'Dad . . .' Ray said slowly, realising what was wrong. 'Where's Waldo?'

CHAPTER 15
BREAKING NEWS JUST IN

Haze shook his head silently. Nim emerged from Ray's bag, looking sadder than ever. Ray suddenly felt awful for getting cross with him about not wanting to fly. She pulled her cloud-cat into her chest. She couldn't imagine losing him.

'We've been at the Council of Forecasters all afternoon,' said Haze. 'I'm not the only one to lose a cloud-creature. Over a hundred Cloud Weatherlings were lined up outside the Council's headquarters for the same reason. All of their cloud-creatures, gone!'

He slumped down on the large sofa. 'Help yourself to some home-made contrail cobbler,' he said, gesturing limply to five trays of the delicious lumpy dessert sitting on a long table in the centre of the room. 'I needed to keep my mind occupied, so I've been baking.'

Ray's heart ached for her dad. She wished she had the answers to reunite him with Waldo . . . to reunite every Cloud Weatherling with their cloud-creatures. Why were they all disappearing? WHERE had they gone?

Nim floated over to the contrail cobbler, burying his head in it and gobbling down mouthfuls at a time. Ray was relieved to see him acting a little more like his old self.

But even though the cobbler smelled amazing, Ray didn't feel hungry. Plus, contrail cobbler *always* gave you terrible wind, and made you fart pink mist trails. Ray's tummy was already in enough of a knot from all the terrible news about the missing cloud-creatures. And the possible return of Tornadia Twist. She was just about to tell her mum and dad about Coo La La's Tornadia news – when the Fizzovision in the corner of the room buzzed loudly then blared out:

PIGEON CLAIMS ANCIENT ROGUE
IS BACK!

'What above Earth?!' cried Cloudia, turning up the volume.

A neatly dressed reporter appeared on screen, beside a small square playing a video on repeat. It showed Coo La La in wing-cuffs, being restrained by two Weather Warriors.

A problematic pigeon by the name of Coo La La barged into the Council of Forecasters HQ just minutes ago. The pigeon claims that Tornadia Twist, an ancient Rogue from over one thousand years ago, is back.

'How ridiculous!' Haze blurted out.

'That pigeon can't be trusted. He once tried to kidnap me!' said Cloudia with a frown.

'But what if Tornadia IS back?' asked Ray quietly.

'Ray, that's utter nonsense,' said Cloudia, looking annoyed.

The weather reporter continued:

Coo La La has been taken into custody and will face charges for trespassing, harassing and lying to the Council, not to mention his involvement with La Blaze DeLight during the attempted destruction of the oldest forest six months ago, for which he has not stood trial.

In other news, the rainfall over England is a growing concern. The Weather Warriors still have not located the Rogue behind this torrential downpour, but believe they could be located in Cornwall.

'That pigeon should be locked away forever,' said Cloudia sternly. Haze nodded in agreement.

But Ray couldn't forget Coo La La's words. *She's back.* What if he WAS telling the truth?

The Fizzovision buzzed again.

MORE BREAKING NEWS JUST IN!

We have just been informed that Valianté, cloud-creature of Flurryweather Floatatious, head of the Council of Forecasters, is GONE. Almost every cloud-creature in the Weatherlands is now MISSING. We must find them soon or the Weatherlands and Earth will be in big trouble.

'What do they mean, BIG trouble?' asked Droplett.

'If cloud-creatures are disconnected from their Weatherlings for too long, they fade away,' said Haze sadly.

'And if the cloud-creatures disappear, that means no more cloud magic,' Snowden added. 'Clouds keep the Earth cool in the day and the ground warm at night. We need cloud magic in the skies for rain magic to work too. Whether we realise it or not, we are ALL connected. Every type of weather influences another. Every Weatherling needs each other, every human needs the Weatherlings, the Earth needs the weather. No weather . . . no Earth.'

The air felt heavy with worry AND the sound of Nim munching through his fourth tray of contrail cobbler.

CREEEEEEAK.

Ray slid sideways, along with everyone and EVERYTHING in the room.

'WHAT ABOVE EARTH IS HAPPENING?' cried Cloudia, grabbing on to the edge of the window ledge.

Ray slid into a bookshelf. It was as if the whole house was leaning at an angle. She managed to drag herself over to the window and peered out.

Ray was used to Cloud Nine's silver lining snapping occasionally. But this time, it wasn't the silver lining that was the problem. The cloud the house was suspended from was almost completely GONE.

'The cloud magic is already disappearing!' she gasped. 'If we don't save the cloud-creatures, we're going to fall out of the sky!'

'It's worse than that,' Snowden called from underneath the rug that had slid on top of him. 'Our whole WORLD relies on cloud magic to stay afloat. The Cloudimulus Suburbs . . . The City of Celestia . . . The WHOLE of the Weatherlands. If cloud magic is no more, then everything will fall apart. The Weatherlands – and the WEATHER as we know it –would be no more.'

'What do we do?' cried Haze.

But his question went unanswered as the rest of Cloud Nine vanished – and the whole house plummeted towards Earth.

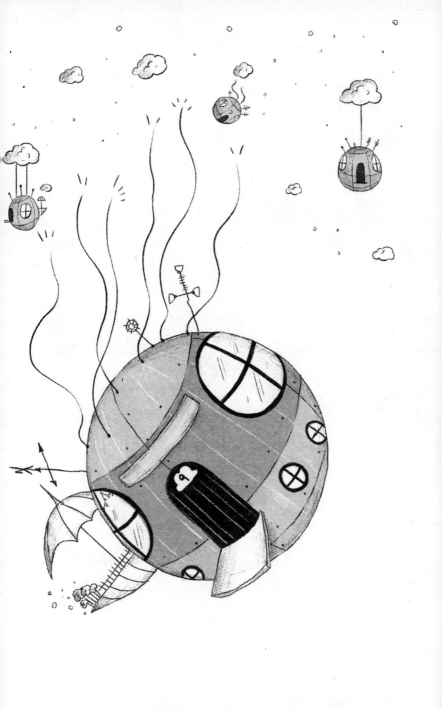

CHAPTER 16

THAT'S NOT VERY NAUGHTY

'If you all hold on to me I might be able to puddle-port us all to safety!' cried Droplett before she got splattered by a tray of contrail cobbler hurtling through the air.

Ray was holding her staff with one hand and her mum with the other. She tried to think of ANY rainbow gift that might be able to prevent her family and friends from becoming pitter patter pancakes, but her brain was both racing and blank all at the same time.

'Ray! Are you doing this?' her dad cried.

Ray blinked. 'Huh?'

They weren't falling any more. Instead, they were soaring horizontally through the air. The house straightened up. Through the window,

Ray saw something big and fluffy beneath them.

'MIAOOOOOOOOOOOOOOOOW!'

'NIM!' Ray cried. Pure joy filled her chest. 'Nim has saved us!'

The enormous cloud-cat carried the round house on his huge body across the bright blue sky, back up towards the Weatherlands. Or what was LEFT of the Weatherlands. The City of Celestia was looking more like an incomplete puzzle than a city, with huge pieces missing. The Flurry Mountains were crumbling, and the Valley of Winds was divided in half.

The Weatherlands were slowly falling apart as the cloud magic disappeared.

Nim flew the house to the edge of the city and landed softly before shrinking to normal cat size again.

'Oh, thank you, Nim!' Ray said, burying her head into his floofy body. 'You're the best.'

Cloudia scooped Ray, Snowden and Droplett into her embrace. 'Kids, I don't want you to leave the house – it's not safe out there,' she

said. 'We're going to make some calls to family and friends to make sure they're OK. Snowden, we will let your Granny Everfreeze know you're with us, and Droplett, I'll let the Trickle Towers orphanage know you're safe.'

Ray spotted her school bag on the other side of the room among the ruined plants and broken ornaments and the remains of her dad's home-made contrail cobbler, which Nim was still happily lapping up. Poking out of the bag was *The Book of Forbidden Forces*.

Ray grabbed it, then beckoned her friends over. 'Follow me,' she whispered.

She led them upstairs to her bedroom (which was now even messier than usual), shut the door firmly and closed the curtains. She sat on the floor and plonked her school bag down.

'Now,' she said. 'You have to promise not to tell ANYONE about what I'm about to show you.'

'Ray, I'm not liking the sound of this,' said Snowden.

'I AM,' grinned Droplett, rubbing her hands.

Ray pulled out *The Book of Forbidden Forces*.

'A book?' Droplett said in disappointment. 'That's not very naughty.'

But Snowden backed away. 'That's not just any book,' he stammered. 'Where did you get that, Ray? It's FORBIDDEN.'

'I'm suddenly WAY more interested,' said Droplett, leaning forward to get a better look. She picked up the thick, leather-bound book. 'Forbidden stuff is always more fun.'

'Shhhhhhhh!' Snowden hissed, snatching the book and shoving it back into Ray's bag. 'Granny Everfreeze told me this book is FULL of powerful spells – far too powerful for a Weatherling to use. Which is why they're FORBIDDEN. A Weatherling caught using any of these spells, or even just reading about them, is sent straight to Precipitory Prison!'

Droplett shuffled back a little. 'Um, Ray? You've already been expelled. Are you planning to go full-on Rogue now? I mean, I understand you've had a bad day, but that's a tad excessive.'

'Don't worry, I don't plan on using this book,'
Ray said. 'I just need to find out about one of the
spells.' She flicked through the pages. 'I kept
seeing this eye symbol. First on a tree next to the
puff pod patch, then on the second-year classroom
door, then on the hat at the arena . . . cloud-
creatures have gone missing from all of
those places.'

'Ray, I believe you,' said Droplett. 'But I
couldn't see an eye on the classroom door.'

'And I couldn't see it on the hat,' said
Snowden.

'It was definitely there,' said Ray, finally

stopping at the page with the picture of the swirly eye. 'Snowden, could you read out what the spell means? My mind is racing too much for me to concentrate.'

Snowden hesitated, then picked up the book and began to read:

The Eye of the Storm is a powerful spell.
When an Eye or number of Eyes are opened,
the spell caster can use their weather magic
from anywhere the Eyes are located.
No matter where the spell caster is based,
they can channel their weather magic through
any of the open Eyes. Only a Weatherling
in the same magic group as the spell caster
can see the Eyes.

Ray gasped. '*Only a Weatherling in the same magic group as the spell caster can see the Eyes . . .*' she repeated. 'That explains why you can't see them, guys. Because the Eyes weren't created by a Rain or a Snow Weatherling.'

Her friends went quiet.

'You realise what that means, Ray?' said Snowdon at last, with a gulp. 'If you are the only one seeing it?'

'The one casting the Eye of the Storm spell has to be another Rainbow Weatherling . . .' Ray said quietly.

'But YOU'RE the only Rainbow Weatherling, Ray,' said Droplett. Her keen expression slowly changed to dread. 'Aren't you?'

'Maybe Coo La La really IS telling the truth,' said Snowden. 'And that means that the person doing this is . . .'

'Tornadia Twist!' the friends chorused together.

CHAPTER 17

SOMETHING IS OFF

'Guys . . . do you think Tornadia could be the one making all the cloud-creatures disappear?!' gasped Ray. 'Only someone as evil as her would do that!'

Snowden's ears erupted with think-flakes. 'That would make sense,' he said. 'The Eye of the Storm spell would explain how she is able to make the cloud-creatures disappear from ALL over the Weatherlands – *the spell caster can use their weather magic from anywhere the Eyes are located.*'

'If we're right, then this is really REALLY bad news, guys,' Ray said anxiously. 'What are we going to do?'

'How do we break the Eye of the Storm spell?' asked
Droplett.

Snowden lifted the book and read aloud:

Only the magic of a whole clan of Weatherlings
can break the spell.
First, one must find the source; The main
Eye of the Storm where the spell was initiated.
Only weather magic used to open the Eye
can be used to close the Eye.
Once the source is found, say these words:

AWAKE BY NIGHT, AWAKE BY DAY.
OPEN EYES FOR A SPELL TO STAY.
BUT ALL COMBINED CAN ALWAYS TRY,
TO BREAK THIS SPELL AND CLOSE THE EYE.

'Wait, so we need a whole clan of Rainbow
Weatherlings to break the spell?' said Droplett.
'Because we don't have that!
Ray can't break the spell alone?'

'You're right, Droplett,' said Snowden.

Ray was quiet for a moment. Her mind was doing roly-polys. 'But guys . . . I DO have a whole clan's worth of magic inside me,' she said slowly. 'So, maybe it's enough to break the spell? We just need to find the source, then I can try.'

Snowden frowned. 'I don't know, Ray . . . clearly a LOT of power is needed to close the Eye. Your magic isn't strong enough. Remember, we're not dealing with ANY magic here. This is forbidden magic. What if . . .' He lowered his gaze. 'What if it's too much for you?'

Ray's mind was racing. 'But what if this is our only hope of saving cloud magic?' she said sadly. 'I have to at least try?'

The friends were silent.

'There HAS to be another way, surely?' said Droplett finally, flicking through *The Book of Forbidden Forces* gingerly.

Ray slumped down on her bed. Something slipped out of her waistcoat pocket. It was the business card from Agent Nephia.

'BUMS!' Ray blurted out.

'OK, Ray has completely lost it,' said Droplett.

'No . . . B.U.M.S. Agent Nephia! If anyone can help us, it'll be her,' said Ray, feeling hopeful again.

She gathered up her bag and *The Book of Forbidden Forces*. The friends ran downstairs, where Cloudia and Haze were still busy checking in with friends and family.

'Mum, Dad! We'll be back in a minute,' said Ray.

'No!' snapped Cloudia. 'You mustn't go outside, it's not safe. Back upstairs please, kids.'

Ray sighed. Nim was STILL busy lapping up every ounce of contrail cobbler he could find on the floor and the walls.

'Nim, we have to go,' she whispered to the hungry floof-feline.

'You've had enough now. Your farts will be leaving pink misty trails for DAYS.'

Ray tried to pick him up, but the cloud-cat hissed loudly and continued to eat.

'What's got into him?' said Droplett, looking shocked.

'Nim's been acting SO strangely lately,' said Ray. 'It must be something to do with the cloud disappearances.'

Nim finally stopped eating, then floated over to Ray. She hugged the cloud-cat to her chest and ran back upstairs with the others.

'What do we do now?' asked Snowden when they were back in Ray's bedroom.

'We sneak out,' said Ray simply.

She pulled out Agent Nephia's B.U.M.S. business card and studied the coordinates before checking them against a map of the Weatherlands stuck to her bedroom wall.

'It's not too far,' she said. 'We just need to get to the other side of the city.'

To Ray's surprise, Nim expanded to the size

of a bed, ready for flight. She jumped on to his back, then turned to Snowden and Droplett.

'Coming?' she said.

Droplett swung herself on to Nim's back. 'I love a bit of danger.'

'Raaay, it's not safe out there,' Snowden protested.

'When has that ever stopped us?' said Ray with a wink.

'Fiiine,' groaned Snowden. 'I guess breaking rules doesn't count if it's almost the end of the weather world as we know it.'

Once Snowden and Droplett were comfortably poised on Nim's floofy back, Ray guided the cloud-cat slowly and quietly out of her bedroom window. 'Let's fly!'

Ray couldn't believe what she was seeing. Their home was disappearing bit by bit beneath them. In the Forest of Fahrenheits, chunks of trees were missing, leaving gaping great holes in the land. Past the Sun Citadel and the Sky Academy, another large section of cloud was breaking away from the edge of the Weatherlands, fading into nothing.

Ray sped Nim up as they made their way to the very far reaches of the City of Celestia, which was thankfully still intact. She noticed a misty pink trail stretching out from Nim's bottom as the contrail cobbler began to kick in.

'At least I won't be able to lose you, Nim,' said Ray in relief.

With all the cloud magic vanishing around them, Ray had no idea how long the floofy cloud-cat had left. She shook her head, trying to shed the scary thought of losing him. She had to focus right now. With Agent Nephia's help, there was a chance they could stop this and save everyone. She was a cloud expert after all!

A set of windmills fizzled into view, the largest at the very top of a cloudy hill. Ray checked the coordinates on the business card against her compass and nodded towards the largest windmill.

'I think this is it,' she said.

Nim landed smoothly on the hill. Ray couldn't help noticing a sad look in his eyes. Perhaps he'd eaten too much food and was on the verge of exploding?

'I didn't think this mill was in use any more,' said Snowden.

'The Bureau of Unexplained Meteorological Sightings is a secret organisation, dealing with secret stuff,' said Ray. 'Maybe this is a temporary base.'

The friends walked slowly up to the mill. Nim followed close behind, back to normal cloud-cat size. There weren't any houses around this area of the city. Wind Weatherlings from Sky Academy often used the smaller windmills for weather magic practice, but otherwise it was deserted.

There was a sudden groaning sound. One of

the small mills began to fall sideways as the land disappeared beneath it. The friends gasped.

'We're running out of time . . . and LAND!' said Ray, running towards the large mill door. 'Quick!'

She knocked urgently. 'Please be here, please be here,' she muttered.

The door opened. Ray let out a sigh of relief. Agent Nephia stood silhouetted by the light of a thousand tiny sunflower lanterns behind her.

'DARLING!' the agent said, looking surprised. Her cloud-crook was perched by the door but there was no sign of the huge cloud-slug.

An awful thought occurred to Ray. 'Mr Steve!' she gasped. 'Is he –'

'Gone, departed, vamooshed,' said Nephia sadly. She shook her head. 'I didn't even get a last hug goodbye.'

'Agent Nephia, we have something REALLY important we need to tell you. Information that might help solve the cloud-creature mystery and help you find Mr Steve!' said Ray.

'Really? Then do come in and tell me ALL,' said the agent.

'Agent Nephia, everything's falling apart. We can't stay here,' said Ray.

But the agent was already inside the mill. Ray and the others followed. It was far bigger inside than it had looked on the outside. A round wooden table and chairs sat in the middle of the room and the walls were decorated in tiny, twinkling sunflower lanterns and LOTS of very elaborate hats.

Agent Nephia gestured to the table. 'I'll fetch some drinks. You must be parched!'

'I don't think we have time for drinks –' Ray started. But the agent had already left the room.

'Do you think Agent Nephia will mind if we tried on some of her hats?' said Droplett. 'If we're gonna fall out of the sky, we should do it in style.'

She picked up the nearest hat. Two giant, feathery sculptures poked out from either side, resembling a HUGE moustache. Droplett popped it on. Her head completely disappeared.

'Droplett! ' said Ray, feeling impatient.
'This is no time for fun. We need to tell Agent
Nephia about Tornadia and get OUT of here
before the whole place falls apart.'

Snowden was frowning. He held out his hand
to Droplett. 'Give me that hat,' he said.

'Pick your own hat!' said Droplett crossly.

Snowden whipped the hat off Droplett's head.
'I knew it,' he said. 'Look!'

Ray and Droplett stared at two sparkly letters -
'S.E.' – on the brim.

'This stands for Sleeta Everfreeze,' gasped
Snowden. 'That's Granny. She ALWAYS initials
the hats she makes for the Greatest Snowman.'

He took another hat off the wall and peered at the brim. 'F.E. . . . Frostanora Everfreeze. That's my great gran. She made *this* hat . . .' He stared around the walls. 'Why would Agent Nephia have all the hats the Everfreeze family gave to the Greatest Snowman?'

Ray felt as if a big block of ice had dropped into her stomach. Her knees buckled beneath her.

'Remember when La Blaze said no one could live as long as a thousand years?' Ray croaked. 'Snowden, how long did you say the Greatest Snowman has been standing for?'

'Around a thousand years,' Snowden replied in barely a whisper.

'Don't you think that's a bit of a coincidence?' said Ray. 'Coo La La claims Tornadia is back after a thousand years, and the Greatest Snowman miraculously melts – *after a thousand years*?'

Nim miaowed sadly. Ray hugged him tightly and gulped. 'Guys, what if . . . what if Tornadia Twist WAS the Greatest Snowman?

What if she was FROZEN for a thousand years?'

'But if Tornadia was the Greatest Snowman, then why does Agent Nephia have all the Everfreeze family hats?' said Droplett.

Ray felt her heart plummet. 'I don't think Agent Nephia is who we think she is. We have to get out of here. NOW.'

Nim miaowed again. Ray stroked his soft head.

'It's OK, Nim,' she said. 'I won't let anything happen to you.'

'I can puddle-port us out,' said Droplett.

The friends each grabbed one of Droplett's arms. Droplett swished her cape. Nothing. She performed a few squats, spun on the spot, then SWISHED again. But not even one drop of rain appeared.

'I . . . I can't use my magic,' said Droplett in a shaky voice. 'This has NEVER happened before!'

Snowden raised a gloved hand to draw a snowflake in the air. But he just looked as though he was pointing to an invisible bug flying around in front of him. He gulped and looked at Ray.

Oh no . . .

Although Rainbow Weatherlings could control other weather magic, they could NOT control another *Rainbow Weatherling*'s magic. It was up to Ray now. She pulled her staff out from her waistcoat.

But Nim miaowed in alarm and was suddenly floating backwards involuntarily towards a dark doorway.

'I wouldn't do anything stupid if I were you, darling . . .'

Agent Nephia appeared with a menacing smile. She took off her long coat and the elaborate hat. Then removed her three pairs of tinted glasses, revealing one purple eye and one blue eye.

Ray felt like the world had stopped. She gulped and said softly, 'Tornadia Twist . . .'

CHAPTER 18

I DO NOT GIVE UP

Tornadia clapped slowly.

'You clever little DARLINGS!' she said. 'Who'd have thought, eh? The Snow Weatherlings have been giving THANKS to Tornadia Twist for ALL these years. What a *twist* in the tale!' She laughed a manic, ear-piercing laugh that echoed around the mill.

'We take ALL our thanks back!' shouted Snowden.

Droplett swished her cape again, but nothing happened. 'GIVE US OUR MAGIC!' she yelled.

Tornadia raised an eyebrow. 'Zip it, darling. You're getting your knickers in such a twist.' She laughed again. 'HA! Twist! Get it?!'

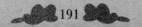

Ray's heart was beating at supersonic speed. She knew that she couldn't take control of Tornadia's magic – that was rainbow lore. But the lore didn't say anything about not being able to use a gift. Ray thought hard. There HAD to be one gift that Ray could use against Tornadia? Something . . . anything! But the truth was, Ray hadn't perfected a single one. Nim was floating next to Tornadia, miaowing miserably. Tornadia was controlling him, just like she was controlling Droplett's magic, and Snowden's magic – using her gift to twist it into whatever weather she liked. If Ray was SUPER fast, maybe just maybe, she could create a rainbow slide and get them out of the mill? She gripped her staff a little tighter.

'Don't do anything silly, Ray,' said Tornadia as if reading her mind. 'You wouldn't want anything to happen to your precious cloud-cat, hmmm?'

Ray loosened her grip. Her heart was aching for poor Nim, still floating by Tornadia's shoulder with a sad expression on his cloudy face.

'Now who fancies a little chat?' said Tornadia

in a jolly tone.

The friends were silent.

'I said, WHO FANCIES A LITTLE CHAT?'
Tornadia roared, lightning sizzling from her
fingertips.

Snowden cleared his throat. 'We don't have
time for a chat. In case you hadn't noticed, the
Weatherlands are falling out of the sky.'

Tornadia tilted her head to one side, then
reached out. Ray felt a gust of wind pull her
towards the table, dragging her into one of
the chairs.

'You could have just ASKED us to sit down!'
growled Droplett as she was also pulled into
a chair.

'Now tell me,' said Tornadia, taking a seat at
the table and cupping her hands around her chin.
'Is it true that there's a whole lesson in school
dedicated to ME?'

'Yes,' said Ray, a sharp edge to her voice.
'But it's *not* our favourite lesson.'

Tornadia put a hand to her chest in mock

offence. 'Darling! That's not a very nice thing to say.'

'And stealing the cloud-creatures isn't a very nice thing to DO!' said Ray. 'Where are they?'

Tornadia raised an eyebrow. 'Drizzling drainpipes. What makes you think I'm the one who's been taking those poor little floofs?'

'Because I've seen the EYES – the *forbidden* magic – in all the places where the cloud-creatures have disappeared,' said Ray.

Tornadia got to her feet and paced the room. Nim followed her helplessly.

'Please let Nim go,' Ray begged.

'No,' Tornadia said casually. 'I like the cat. Plus, he's super fun to shapeshift.'

She made a fist and Nim slowly turned into a cloud-slug.

Ray gasped. 'Mr Steve!'

It suddenly made sense. Nim had ALWAYS exploded whenever Nephia/Tornadia was around. The evil Rogue had been using her magic to change Nim's shape all along, making it LOOK

like she had her own cloud-creature!

'Turn him back!' Ray shouted, leaping to her feet.

'Calm your stripy socks, darling, I'm just having some FUN. Do you even know what that is?' said Tornadia with a light chuckle. She waved a hand and the cloud-slug turned back into Nim again. 'You always assume the worst of me.'

'That's because you ARE the worst!' shouted Droplett. 'You eliminated ALL the rainbow weather magic a thousand years ago *and* made a storm that lasted a hundred years!'

Tornadia rolled her eyes. 'Is everyone STILL moaning about that? You'd think they'd be over it by now.'

She spun on the spot, creating a mini whirlwind around her ankles, allowing her to glide across the room.

'I used to be just like you, Ray,' she said casually.

'We're *nothing* alike!' Ray snapped.

'YEAH! Ray doesn't have black and white stripy hair,' Droplett added.

'Multicoloured hair is *so* ten centuries ago,' said Tornadia. 'When you dabble with forbidden magic it has some side effects. But I rather like it.' She patted the underside of her swirly monotone hair.

Ray tried to look as mighty as possible. 'We're going to tell the Council of Forecasters about you and then you'll be sorry you ever came back to the Weatherlands.'

Tornadia burst out laughing. 'You won't be telling anyone about ANYTHING, darling,'

She lifted her left hand, fingers spread, before slowly making a fist shape. Nim began to disappear.

'STOP IT!' Ray yelled.

But Nim had gone. Ray felt like her whole world had stopped.

'Your precious Nim will be fine, just like all the other cloud-creatures. As long as you don't do anything *silly*,' said Tornadia, her purple and blue eyes flashing with darkness. 'Now sit yourself back down so we can *chat* like civilised Weatherlings, hmm?'

Tornadia perched on the edge of the chair and laced her fingers together, gently placing her hands in her lap. 'I meant it when I said I was just like you, Ray. All I wanted to do was *help*.'

Ray couldn't even respond. She focused on the empty space where Nim had vanished.

'Weatherlings are miraculous creatures,' Tornadia continued. 'They work HARD to bring the most spectacular displays of weather to the world.'

Ray was surprised to find herself agreeing with something Tornadia said.

'BUT Weatherlings are *never* appreciated,' added the Rogue. 'All they do is work day and night to make the human Earth a better place. But those humans don't CARE. They complain no matter what.'

Tornadia conjured a burning ball of light in front of her, making it glow brighter and brighter.

'It's always too hot, too wet, too windy!' Tornadia sent a gust of wind sweeping through the mill. 'The humans are NEVER happy. They are ungrateful little windsocks. I watched one of my BEST friends, Drizella Pipe, create the most wonderful misty rain one fine day over Paris. She was the BEST Rain Weatherling out there, in my opinion. But then I overheard a spiteful little child singing "*RAIN RAIN GO AWAY, come again another day*" . . . Drizella was so upset. She did NOT deserve that. So, I took control of Drizella's rain magic and created the BIGGEST water-serpent I possibly could.' She chuckled.

'THAT gave the rotten little human a reason to complain.'

Ray put her head in her hands. 'You can't DO that, Tornadia.'

'Humans LIKE to complain about the weather,' Snowden added. 'It gives them something to talk about.'

Tornadia's expression turned dark and a deep rumble of thunder shook the mill.

'You think I'm just a Rogue,' she said.

'But I once tried to HELP others. I used my rainbow weather magic to stop a whole army of snowmen from trampling on the king of Norway. I froze the snowmen and turned them into a wonderful ice sculpture. Then I overheard the king say it was the UGLIEST thing he'd ever seen and he couldn't wait for it to melt. So, I froze his ungrateful royal bottom to his THRONE.'

The whole mill shuddered. A large crack stretched across the ground. The wind outside was picking up.

'The whole of the Weatherlands looked at me as if I was some kind of criminal after that, when all I did was STICK UP for them.' Tornadia's expression was fierce. 'THAT'S the thanks I get! For *helping*. But it's fine. I didn't NEED them. The Rogues understood me when nobody else did.' Her blue and purple eyes were wide and wild. 'They introduced me to *The Book of Forbidden Forces*. That taught me all about Shadow Essence and what it could do. THERE was my answer.'

'But why take away all the rainbow weather magic?' shouted Ray, trying to make herself heard above the howling wind.

'Without their magic, they were no threat to me,' said Tornadia darkly. 'BUT there was only ever one Rainbow Weatherling I was bothered about, because he had the most POWERFUL of all the rainbow gifts . . . Rainbow Beard.'

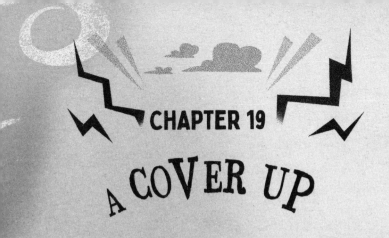

CHAPTER 19

A COVER UP

'Rainbow *Beard*?' said Ray.

'How above Earth is he your BIGGEST threat?' scoffed Droplett. 'What could he do? Wrap you up in a load of colourful facial hair?'

'His gift has nothing to do with beards,' said Tornadia scornfully. 'The name Rainbow BEARD was just a cover-up.'

Snowden gasped. 'Just like a REAL beard covers a chin!'

That explained why La Blaze had never been able to find anything about Rainbow Beard's special gift in the Rainburrow.

'So what WAS Rainbow Beard's gift?' asked Ray.

Tornadia hit the table with her fist. There was a fizzle of lightning and a great rumble of thunder, making Ray and the friends jump.

'That's for me to know and you to NEVER find out,' Tornadia hissed.

Ray could *feel* the electricity in the air.

'I couldn't risk Rainbow Beard using his gift on me all those years ago,' said the Rogue. 'I *had* to eliminate it. But, in an attempt to protect me from the Shadow Essence I had unleashed, one of my Snow Rogues used too much magic and froze me solid! That's the last thing I remember . . .' She grinned. 'But I can thank RAY here for helping to break me free from my thousand-year-long sleep.'

Ray stiffened. 'I didn't *help* you!'

'Oh, but you did,' said Tornadia. 'On every Eclipse, weather magic is at its strongest. That's why YOU were able to unlock the rainbow weather magic that had been trapped inside that crystal for so long. The reintroduction of rainbow weather magic in the world awoke the rainbow weather magic inside ME. All weather is connected, after all. I was FINALLY able to free myself from inside the "Greatest Snowman". If it hadn't been for you,

I'd still be stuck in a big, frozen ball, collecting silly hats.'

Ray went cold.

'That's right,' purred Tornadia. 'YOU helped ME!' She laughed maniacally. 'I had no idea I'd been frozen for a thousand years. I thought my biggest threat was finally gone. Then I heard about you, darling. A ten-year-old Weatherling with no magic, who found a black lump of rock and received *all* the rainbow weather magic I had worked so hard to eliminate. And ALL the rainbow gifts, including Rainbow Beard's. So that makes YOU my biggest threat.'

Ray didn't even know what Rainbow Beard's mysterious gift WAS. How could she be a threat to Tornadia? She looked at her friends and felt an overwhelming sense of guilt. She'd dragged them into this whole mess, and now they were in Tornadia's grip too.

'Why bother disguising yourself as Agent Nephia all this time?' said Droplett coldly.

'I like to plan a villainous return properly,'

Tornadia replied with a shrug.

'I KNEW it,' said Snowden.

'And I needed to figure you out, Ray darling. Gain your trust,' the Rogue continued. 'I also needed to build up my strength after a thousand years frozen inside a snowman. Do you know how detrimental that can be to your JOINTS? My knees haven't been the same since. But I also had a fabulous idea.'

Tornadia walked around the table, stopping behind Ray. 'You and I are VERY special, darling. But nobody else sees that. I can train you. Rainbow to Rainbow.'

She leaned down so that her mouth was level with Ray's ear. The hairs on the back of Ray's neck prickled.

'I understand what it's like to be looked at differently,' Tornadia whispered. 'Feeling like no matter what you do, it's not enough. But a Rainbow Weatherling doesn't need ANYONE! The Earth can be our playground. WE can be the most powerful Weatherlings of them all.'

She held out a hand. 'So, what do you say?'

Ray didn't move. The truth was, she HAD
felt like nobody understood her lately. All she'd
wanted to do was help, but she had only made
things worse. And now Tornadia was back . . .
and it was all her fault.

Ray felt her eyes fill with tears. Following
in Tornadia's footsteps would be giving up on
everything she'd ever believed in. And if there
was ONE thing Ray didn't do, it was give up.

'Do you always take this long to reply?'
asked Tornadia. She tapped Ray's head twice.
'Hellooo?'

'I want nothing to do with you,' said Ray coldly. 'Rainbow Weatherlings do NOT work alone.'

Tornadia's hand dropped to her side. 'You poor thing,' she said calmly. 'What a *terrible* decision.' She moved her hands around in circular motions and rose from the ground, a fierce tornado surrounding her lower body like a nightmarish mermaid's tail. 'You clearly don't know greatness when you see it.'

Ray stood firm. 'I see no greatness here. It's the job of the Weatherlings to keep the Earth and skies in balance,' she said calmly. 'And it's *especially* the job of a Rainbow Weatherling to keep that peace. If everyone did what they pleased, there'd be chaos. The Weatherlands are dying because we are losing our cloud-magic. No Weatherlands means no weather . . . and no Earth.'

'Darling, there WILL be weather. Just not the kind YOU like,' said Tornadia. 'I plan on making this place a storm planet, just like our good friend

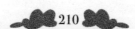

Jupiter. It's Rogue Central there! No humans to worry about. NO RULES. Just free weather! Beautiful CHAOS.'

Tornadia sent a rush of wind towards the ceiling. There was a creaking sound as the mill's large wind turbines began to turn slowly. She pushed her hands forward and up, sending Snowden and Droplett flying out through one of the high windows of the mill.

'NO!' cried Ray.

Tornadia grinned and disappeared in a flash of lightning and an ear-piercing clap of thunder.

Ray gripped her staff and felt the magic flood through her veins. Her breathing was fast and shallow . . . she had to focus if she was going to use her magic to escape and save her friends. But something was seeping through the cracks of the walls. Something dark.

'Shadow Essence!' Ray gasped.

Black tendrils weaved their way towards her. If the Shadow Essence touched her, she would lose her magic again – perhaps forever.

She tugged at the door handle, but it was locked. She was trapped!

Ray raced up the staircase, the Shadow Essence tentacles following close behind, until she reached the very top window of the mill. She couldn't go any further. She leaned out of the window – and immediately recoiled when she saw how high she was. How could she escape? And where were Snowden and Droplett?

Something caught her attention. A bright glowing Eye on the ceiling.

'YOU know what it's like to be pushed aside, Ray . . . To have nobody want your magic, or appreciate that all you were trying to do was HELP . . .'

Tornadia's voice echoed around the whole mill. Ray tried not to listen. But the voice filled her head like a dark cloudy headache.

'Have you ever tried SO hard to make people happy and got NOTHING in return but disapproval?'

Ray thought back to the puff pod party,

and all the awful things her Aunt Foggaleena had said. The way Miss Myst dismissed everything Ray tried to say or do. Alto Wisp's face in the Weather Wobblers arena. She had been expelled just because she'd tried to help. She swallowed hard. Ray absolutely *hated* the fact that a TINY part of her could see where Tornadia was coming from.

Listlessly she tried to use her magic to make a rainbow slide and escape. But the colours disappeared as fast as she summoned them. She felt . . . hollow.

The Shadow Essence wrapped itself around her ankles and her wrists, seeping into her soul. She could feel her magic draining away. She tried to move, but her limbs felt like huge, heavy ice blocks. She tried to call out, but couldn't.

Then she saw something. A wispy pink trail zigzagging across the sky. It was the last thing she saw before a blinding light filled her vision.

CHAPTER 20

FLYING

Ray felt a rush of wind in her hair, a warmth on her skin. Then a TAP TAP TAP on her head. She blinked a few times and opened her eyes, before sitting up. The Forest of Fahrenheits was below her.

Ray blinked again and saw Snowden and Droplett's faces. They hugged her tight.

'RAY!' said a familiar voice. 'Thank the skies!'

Ray then realised she was flying upon a bright yellow dragon. There was only one Weatherling who could create a sun-dragon like that.

'La Blaze!' cried Ray with joy.

'You still got your magic, kid?' La Blaze asked, looking concerned.

Ray grabbed her staff, feeling the colours rush through her and the familiar tingle in her

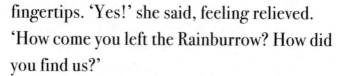

fingertips. 'Yes!' she said, feeling relieved. 'How come you left the Rainburrow? How did you find us?'

'The Weatherlands is falling apart,' said La Blaze, the sunlight reflecting off her bright lemon hair. 'I couldn't just sit underground. I came out to help Weatherlings get to safety. Then I saw your house on the ground, near the city. Your parents were worried sick because you three had disappeared . . . Luckily I spotted a pink contrail in the sky, stretching from your bedroom window. I knew it had to be from Nim. You've always told me how much he loves contrail cobbler. I followed the trail and saw Droplett and Snowdon being swept through the skies inside a huge tornado. That's when I knew something was wrong. They filled me in on the rest . . .' La Blaze shook her head. 'Agent Nephia, eh?'

'I know,' said Ray. 'I trusted her! La Blaze, I can't thank you enough for saving me, but surely you're risking a life sentence in Precipitory Prison if you're caught outside?'

La Blaze laughed. 'That's the LEAST of my concerns right now. Anyway, I'd risk it all to help you save the cloud-creatures and the Weatherlands. Don't you worry about what happens to me.'

'But –'

La Blaze held up a hand. 'No buts!' she said firmly. She winked. 'As the only adult here, I FORBID you to stop me.'

Ray didn't know what to say. She threw her arms around La Blaze's waist. La Blaze really WAS her hero.

Nim's pink misty trail stretched out before them, across the Weatherlands and beyond the horizon. All around them, Wind Weatherlings were trying desperately to keep houses and building afloat using their magic. Snow Weatherlings had generated temporary icy platforms where huge chunks of cloud had once stood. Weather Warriors were getting stranded Weatherlings to safety as more chunks of land slowly vanished beneath them.

Ray desperately wanted to help. But the only way to do that was to find the cloud-creatures and restore cloud magic once and for all.

As Ray focused on the pink trail ahead of them, her own words to Nim before entering Tornadia's trap replayed in her head: '*At least I won't be able to lose you . . .*'

A brilliant idea struck her.

'Guys,' she gasped. 'If we follow Nim's pink trail, maybe we'll find him and all the other cloud-creatures Tornadia has been hiding? She said he'd be safe, *just like all the other cloud-creatures.*'

'Nim did eat a LOT of contrail cobbler,' said Snowden. 'Enough to leave a trail for miles!'

'Nim *knew* he was going to get taken away,' Ray said quietly. 'I think he ate all the cobbler so we could find him and the other cloud-creatures!'

Her voice broke and her eyes prickled with tears. Droplett and Snowden both hugged her tight.

'Nim's always been a clever kitty!' said Droplett.

'We'll bring him back home Ray, no matter what it takes,' said Snowden gently.

'Well, we'd better hurry,' said La Blaze. 'Otherwise we won't have a home to come back to.'

Another huge chunk of cloud disappeared from the edges of the Weatherlands, taking most of the Forest of Fahrenheits with it.

Ray wiped her tears. 'We need to find the cloud-creatures and restore the cloud magic, QUICK!' she said. 'So, let's follow that contrail!'

La Blaze leaned forward into the sun-dragon until the sunflowers on her wrists shone even brighter. Then she guided them all across the skies, and all the way down to Earth, following Nim's trail.

Rain began to pour so it became harder to see. Eventually the friends skidded to a halt on a sandy beach. Weatherlings became visible to humans when they touched solid ground, but luckily nobody was around. La Blaze clicked her fingers and the sun-dragon got smaller and smaller until it was a ball of light in the palm of her hand.

'This is where Nim's trail leads us,' La Blaze yelled through the pounding rain. 'England! Wow, this place is WET.'

'England? This must be the weird rain Dad
was talking about!' gasped Ray. 'The Weather
Warriors couldn't find the Rain Rogue behind it.'

It was raining so hard that Ray could barely see
anything, apart from rocks surrounding a large,
dark cave.

Droplett lifted her arms and stuck her tongue
out. She frowned. 'Something's not right about
this rain,' she said. 'I know my rain . . . and this
doesn't feel normal.'

Snowden removed his glasses. 'But . . . it's so
WET. It feels like real rain to me.'

Ray looked around desperately for any further
signs of Nim's contrail. 'Niiiiim!' she called out.

'RAY!' Droplett yelled. 'LOOK!'

Droplett was staring at one of the large puddles of water on the sodden sand. Ray rushed over. She looked down – and couldn't believe what she was seeing.

Instead of her own reflection in the puddle . . .

Two tiny eyes were gazing back at her!

CHAPTER 21

TWIST!

'NIM?' she cried, half happy, half baffled. 'Why is Nim in a *puddle*?'

There was an eruption of think-flakes from Snowden's ears. 'TWIST!' he gasped. 'Remember we read about Tornadia's rainbow gift – she has the ability to *twist* one weather into another!'

The puzzle pieces fell into place.

'Tornadia turned the cloud-creatures into rain! The cloud-creatures ARE the rain!' Ray shouted hysterically. 'Then she hid them on Earth . . . We've FOUND them!' She spun around on the spot. 'That's why Nim's trail ended here and that's why my dad couldn't find the Rogue responsible. Because it was never real rain in the first place!' She looked back at the puddle. 'Oh, Nim, I'm so sorry this happened to you.

I'm going to save you, don't worry.'

Nim's face was pushed to one side as another large puddle slid over with a recognisable and very grumpy face inside.

'Waldo!' said Ray with a giggle, her eyes full of tears.

'MIAOW!' the Nim puddle said with a smile, before sliding along the sand.

'Nim?' said Ray, giving chase.

The puddle skimmed along the beach, heading into the dark cave.

'Guys!' Ray called. 'I think Nim's trying to show us something.'

Snowden, Droplett and La Blaze clambered across the jagged rocks after Ray, careful not to tread in the cloud-creature puddles. They were absolutely EVERYWHERE as the friends entered the cave together.

Instead of getting darker inside the cave, it got lighter. Then . . .

Ray came face to face with a large, glowing symbol. She stopped dead.

An Eye of the Storm.

'What's up, Ray?' asked Droplett.

'It's one of the Eyes,' said Ray. 'And it's HUGE! It must be the source of the Forbidden Spell.'

The swirly Eye glowed furiously, pulsing with POWER. Ray swallowed hard.

She pulled *The Book of Forbidden Forces* from her bag. 'I have to try to close the Eye and break the spell,' she said firmly.

'Ray,' Snowden said uncomfortably. 'Please don't do this . . .'

'What's going on?' asked La Blaze.

'Only the magic of a whole clan of Rainbow Weatherlings can break the spell,' said Droplett. 'But Ray wants do it by herself . . .'

'No, kid —' La Blaze started.

'I have a whole clan's worth of magic inside me,' urged Ray. 'I have to try! I'm our only hope.'

The only sound was the thrashing rain against the rocks and a sad miaow from Nim.

La Blaze took Ray's hand. Her large crystal

eyes were wide and glossy. 'It's too risky, kid. Your life only just got started.'

'If I break the spell, then cloud magic will be saved. The Weatherlands would be whole again!' said Ray.

'And what if the forbidden magic is too strong to break?' asked La Blaze. 'Then what?'

Silence. Ray didn't need to say it out loud. She knew what would happen.

Ray looked at her friends. She couldn't imagine never seeing Snowden and Droplett again, or her hero La Blaze, or her mum and dad . . . or Nim. Sweet, wonderful Nim.

But if Ray didn't do this, then the Weatherlands were no more. She had to do this for them. For everyone she loved.

'I'm the only one who can break the spell. I have to at least try,' Ray said softly. 'There's no other way.'

CHAPTER 22
SNORBS

Snowden threw his arms around Ray. 'There HAS to be another way!' he sobbed into her shoulder. Think-flakes were pouring from his ears and nostrils. 'Give me some time to think of something – *anything*!'

Droplett hugged Ray. 'Snow-boy's right,' she sniffed. 'There MUST be something else we can do.'

Outside, there was a deep rumble of thunder. The wind was picking up.

'Uh-oh,' said La Blaze.

Ray felt a shiver run down her spine. She stuffed *The Book of Forbidden Forces* into her bag. They couldn't afford to lose it now! Thunder shook the walls. Bright lightning flashed, revealing the silhouette of a figure at the

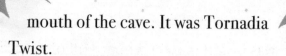

mouth of the cave. It was Tornadia
Twist.

Ray dug her staff into the ground, then lifted
it up and spun round before plunging it into the
ground again. At the same time, colours flooded
her vision and a ball of light erupted from the end
of the staff. There was an almighty POP! – and
the friends found themselves inside a huge
rainbow bubble.

Tornadia's arms were outstretched. Her
rainbow weather magic streamed through the air
in a river of black and grey stripes, totally unlike
the colourful rainbows Ray created. The stripes
rebounded off the protective bubble Ray had
summoned. It had worked!

'You think you can beat ME?' cried Tornadia
in a rage.

She sent the rainbow bubble crashing into the
side of the cave. The friends tumbled over each
other, but Ray held on to her staff tight. Her head
was sore, her limbs were aching, but she would
not let go. Everything she loved was at stake.

HOLD ON, Ray told herself. *Do not give up*. There was bright flash as a huge ball of light BONKED Tornadia on the head.

'Sorry not sorry!' said La Blaze. She turned to Ray and winked. 'Classic sun orb. Or should I say – SNORB!'

'Did you just . . . SNORB ME?' shrieked Tornadia.

BONK! BONK! BONK!

Another ball of sunlight hit Tornadia between the eyes. Then another on the chin, knocking her backwards.

'Isn't this FUN?' sang La Blaze, juggling more sun orbs in her hands.

Tornadia screamed and sent a huge bolt of lightning hurtling through the air towards them. 'YOU DARE SNORB MY FABULOUS HEAD?'

BONK!

'RIGHT IN THE HAIR!' cheered La Blaze.

Ray held on to her staff tightly. As long as she kept the rainbow bubble of protection going, she and her friends were protected from Tornadia's dark magic.

'Keep distracting Tornadia!' Ray shouted to her friends. 'Snowden! See if you can trap her in some ice blocks!' If they could just hold Tornadia for long enough, that would give Ray a chance to break the Eye of the Storm spell.

Snowden drew a snowflake in the air. The snowflake began sweeping towards Tornadia, who was still getting BIFFED in the head with glowing orbs of sunshine.

Droplett swished her cape as hard as she could.

SPLOSH!

Not expecting this damp greeting, Tornadia stumbled backwards. She tried to get up, but lumps of ice had frozen her hands and feet to the ground, thanks to Snowden. She went red in the face.

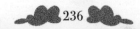

'You think your puny magic can stop me?' she roared. 'You can't hide inside that little bubble of yours forever!'

The ice blocks around her hands and feet shattered into a thousand razor-sharp pieces.

Tornadia was right, though. Ray wasn't sure how much longer the bubble could last. She was growing tired. Her hands were sore from gripping her staff so tightly. There HAD to be something else Ray could do. She spotted the cloud-creature puddles sliding around the walls of the cave and suddenly had a brilliant idea.

'Puddles . . .' Ray muttered to herself. If she could take control of Droplett's magic, perhaps Ray could PUDDLE-PORT Tornadia away! That would give Ray enough time to finally break the forbidden spell . . . But first, she needed to distract Tornadia long enough to burst the bubble of protection and get control of the rain magic.

'GUYS. I need you to do EXACTLY what I say . . . This is our only hope. Droplett, I'm going to need to borrow your magic, OK?'

'Of course!' Droplett replied, spreading her arms out with a grin. 'My rain is your rain.'

'Snowden, I need you to take *The Book of Forbidden Forces* out of my bag and open it to the Eye of the Storm page!'

Snowden's face was full of concern. But he bowed his head and slipped the book from Ray's bag.

Then Ray shouted, 'La Blaze! I need you to

create the BIGGEST SNORB you can. But don't throw it at Tornadia!'

La Blaze saluted. 'You got it, kid!' She squeezed her fists. Her sunflower wristbands glowed brightly, creating a HUGE ball of sunlight.

'BIGGER!' cried Ray. Her grip on her staff was slipping. Before long the bubble of protection would pop.

La Blaze made the glowing ball bigger. The whole cave lit up as if it were daytime. Tornadia blasted lightning bolt after lightning bolt at the bubble. Every hit weakened Ray's hold, and Tornadia knew it. But Ray just needed to hang on for a little longer. She wasn't scared any more. She was DETERMINED.

'BIGGER! BRIGHTER!' Ray shouted again.

'Ray, if La Blaze makes it any brighter, it's going to blind us!' said Snowden.

'Close your eyes! Make it brighter, La Blaze!'

La Blaze looked hesitant but nodded, using
her sun magic to make the ball glow brighter still.
Ray squinted in the dazzling light. She could see
Tornadia falter, shielding her face. Snowden and
Droplett covered their eyes with their hands.

'BRIGHTER!' Ray cried again. The light was
searing. Her temples were dripping with sweat.
Her hand was slipping on her staff. Ray REALLY
hoped her plan would work. She was almost ready.

'But Ray –'

'Just TRUST me. BRIGHTER! QUICK.'

La Blaze let out a yell as her sun magic poured
through her sunflower wristbands. Ray's eyes were

closed tight, but the light shone through
her eyelids.

She heard Tornadia cursing. There was a skid
and a bomp, then a splosh. It sounded like
Tornadia had lost her balance.

This was Ray's only chance to get this right.
She loosened her grip on her staff. The rainbow
bubble disappeared, exposing her friends,
tempting Tornadia to take their magic. With her
eyes still closed, Ray pointed her staff towards
where she knew Droplett was standing.

Ray let her rainbow weather magic pour out
through her fingertips, through the staff and
towards her friend. Within seconds she felt
a familiar tug . . . a rush of rain. Ray now had
control of Droplett's rain magic.

The sunlight disappeared. Ray slowly opened her eyes, her vision still filled with the bright white light as if it had been printed into her mind.

Tornadia's arms were outstretched. A black and grey striped rainbow engulfed the friends, wrapping around them like rope.

'You think you're so clever . . .' Tornadia snarled. 'You're WEAK.'

She conjured up a lightning bolt and threw it towards Ray.

'RAY!' cried Snowden.

Ray remembered Droplett's words: *The secret to great puddle-porting is POISE and relaxation. Let the puddle take you . . .*

Ray took a deep breath. It was as if the world was moving in slow motion. She let her whole body relax, then pointed her staff at her feet where a huge puddle appeared. With one great SPLOSH, Ray disappeared into the puddle, narrowly missing the incoming bolt of bright green lightning. Seconds later she emerged from *another* puddle behind Tornadia, making sure to SPLOSH her very hard upon arrival.

'YESSSSSS, RAY!' cheered Droplett. 'You're using my magic like a PRO PUDDLE-PORTER!'

Tornadia spun round. 'You little RAINBOW WRETCH,' she spat.

Ray didn't break eye contact. She stared at Tornadia. Stared into those deep purple and blue eyes so like her own. Ray found it hard to believe that Tornadia was a Rainbow Weatherling too – they couldn't be more different.

Tornadia roared and prepared to launch her magic at Ray. But Ray flicked her staff – and with one almighty PLOP, Tornadia disappeared into a puddle of water beneath her. Ray then closed the puddle portal, and there was silence.

CHAPTER 23

THE SPELL

'No . . . way . . .' said Droplett.

'KID, YOU ARE A GENIUS!' bellowed
La Blaze.

But Ray knew it wasn't over yet. Wherever
Tornadia was, she wouldn't stay there for long.
She looked to Snowden and nodded once. He held
out the *The Book of Forbidden Forces* opened to
the Eye of the Storm spell. She tried to focus on
the words . . . but the letters were jumping around
frantically. She needed to remain calm and take
each word at a time.

'Ray . . . what if it's too powerful. Too much
for you?' asked Snowden weakly.

'It's a risk I have to take,' Ray replied firmly.
'We have no other choice.'

She didn't have time to dwell. The Weatherlands were falling apart and only Ray could stop it. Only Ray could save the cloud magic. Plus, if she thought about it too much, there was a risk she'd get too scared. She couldn't afford to let everyone down. Ray turned and pointed her staff towards the large glowing Eye at the back of the cave. As her magic surged through it she began to read the words to break the spell:

AWAKE BY NIGHT, AWAKE BY DAY.
OPEN EYES FOR A SPELL TO STAY.
BUT ALL COMBINED CAN ALWAYS TRY,
TO BREAK THIS SPELL AND CLOSE THE EYE.

The Eye in the cave was still glowing wide and bright.

Ray's head was aching and her body was trembling as her magic pulsed through her veins. Her fingers were tingling furiously, and her mouth was dry.

'Ray! STOP! It's too powerful!' shouted Droplett.

Ray could FEEL her colour draining away – from her hair, from her veins, from her soul. Every ounce of her rainbow weather magic was pouring into the Eye of the Storm.

She HAD to break the spell. NO matter the cost.

There was an almighty rumble. The cave walls were shaking. As Ray poured her magic through the Eye she could FEEL Tornadia's power, which had kept the Eyes glowing for all this time.

Then, to Ray's horror, a voice pierced her mind.

'You should have joined me when you had the chance!' screamed Tornadia, her voice filled with cruel laughter. 'You think you can make a difference? One lonely little Rainbow Weatherling? You have ALL that power and you're throwing it away on a feeble little planet that doesn't care!'

'You're wrong,' gasped Ray. 'I'm not alone.

I have everyone in the skies and on Earth.' She felt her legs wobble. 'And I will do ALL it takes to protect them.'

Ray felt Snowden and Droplett put a hand on each of her shoulders, filling her with hope and strength. La Blaze placed her hands around Ray too, her sun magic filling Ray with warmth.

'We're right here with you, Ray,' said La Blaze.

Ray stood firm. She could do this!

'Rainbows are more than a band of colours, Tornadia,' she said. 'They are a symbol of hope, unity and LOVE.'

'EURGH. So booooring!' Tornadia bellowed. 'I'm Tornadia Twist. Future storm queen. And JUST like you, Ray, I'm no quitter.'

Ray was so tired. The evil magic of the Eye was consuming her. But as she fell to her knees, she saw the puddle at her feet, lapping gently at her ankles.

It was Nim, and he was smiling.

Seeing her beloved cloud-cat gave Ray one

final bit of strength to choke out the magic
words one more time:

AWAKE BY NIGHT. AWAKE BY DAY.
OPEN EYES FOR A SPELL TO STAY.
BUT ALL COMBINED CAN ALWAYS TRY,
TO BREAK THIS SPELL AND CLOSE THE EYE.

Ray saw the Eye on the tree, the Eye on the classroom door, the Eye on the hat. She caught glimpses of Eyes all around the Weatherlands, showing how Tornadia had been able to control and steal the cloud-creatures from anywhere and EVERYWHERE.

Tornadia screamed with rage as the glow of the Eye started to fade. And Ray felt Tornadia's presence leave her as the Eye finally closed, plunging them into darkness.

The Forbidden Spell was broken.

Everything went quiet.

CHAPTER 24

THE AURORA

Ray opened her eyes slowly. It was still dark, apart from a greeny-pink shimmer at the edge of her vision. She sat up. The ground beneath her was softer than a cloud. When she looked down she realised there was absolutely *nothing* beneath her. Just a VAST space between Ray's bottom and Earth way *way* down below.

She wasn't sure what else to do, so she screamed.

'Oh, hello!' said a voice.

Ray whipped her head around. There was a group of people sitting at a long table in front of her, having some kind of tea party.

'How long have you been here?' said a man with an incredibly long beard.

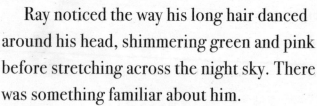

Ray noticed the way his long hair danced around his head, shimmering green and pink before stretching across the night sky. There was something familiar about him.

'Are you . . . a ghost?' Ray asked.

'I guess you could call it that,' said the bearded man. He smiled kindly. 'We're all friendly ghosts, though. We are family, after all.'

Ray suddenly knew why she recognised him. 'Rainbow Beard?' she said, taking his hand. She gasped, for her own hand was just like his. 'Am I a ghost, too?'

'For now,' said Rainbow Beard.

Ray heard singing.

Return again, you'll be OK,
What's mine is yours. You're here to stay.

'Can I interest you in a cup of Borealis broth?' asked Rainbow Beard, pointing towards the table of ghostly Weatherlings, who all seemed to be having a very jolly tea party.

'I should really get home,' said Ray. 'I think I was in the middle of saving the world.'

'Goodness,' said Rainbow Beard. 'Sounds like a busy afternoon.'

The table of ghosts waved at Ray. She recognised some of their faces from the books and pictures of ancient Rainbow Weatherlings in the Rainburrow. Like Rainbow Beard, their hair was also made of the green and pink lights that danced and wiggled across the night sky.

Ray gasped. 'Your hair looks just like the Aurora Borealis . . .'

'Ah, yes,' said Rainbow Beard, pulling out a chair for Ray. 'Have you ever wondered what the Aurora Borealis really is? Every Rainbow Weatherling eventually joins the Aurora. And one day, you will dance here with us too.'

Ray lifted a lock of her own hair. It looked like silky water, stretching across the sky with the Aurora hair of the other Rainbow Weatherlings, creating the most beautiful display of Northern Lights.

Ray couldn't quite believe she was with her family from the past. Part of her wanted to stay with them. But her family and friends from the *present* would be worried sick about her. And Nim . . . poor Nim . . .

'It isn't your time yet,' said Rainbow Beard, as if reading her mind.

'It isn't?' asked Ray.

She heard the singing again. She KNEW that voice.

Return again, you'll be OK,
What's mine is yours. You're here to stay.

'You have Weatherlings who love you very much,' said Rainbow Beard gently. 'Weatherlings who are willing to do anything to make sure you're OK.'

Why did Ray's feet feel so tingly? She looked down and realised she could hardly see them.

'What's happening?' she gasped.

'You're going back home,' said Rainbow

Beard. 'Seems like your friends haven't given up on you. Just like you didn't give up on them.' He smiled. 'Never give up on yourself, Rainbow Grey. Embrace your differences. Your rainbow weather magic will take years to master, but one day you'll unlock our gifts.'

'But what if the Weatherlands don't accept me after everything Tornadia has done?' Ray said anxiously. 'Will they ever be able to trust rainbow weather magic?'

'Tornadia Twist does NOT speak for ALL Rainbow Weatherlings,' said Rainbow Beard. 'A Rainbow Weatherling represents all that is good. All that is love.'

Ray's hands were fading now. But there was one more question she had to ask.

'Rainbow Beard, what does YOUR unique gift do? Tornadia said it was a secret gift, the most powerful of them all.'

There was a glint in Rainbow Beard's purple eye. 'She is right,' he said. 'My true gift had to be concealed from those who might try to abuse it.'

'But what IS it?' asked Ray, aware that she was now just a floating head.

But she didn't hear Rainbow Beard's reply. Everything went dark once again.

'Ray?' said a voice.

Ray opened her eyes slowly. Filling her vision were four of her favourite faces. Snowden, Droplett, La Blaze – and NIM!

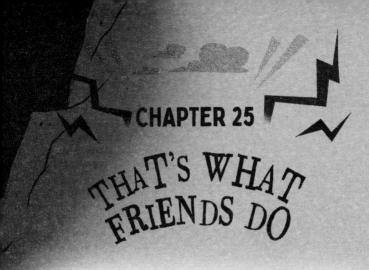

CHAPTER 25

THAT'S WHAT FRIENDS DO

Ray found herself being hugged so tight she could hardly breathe.

'You're ALIVE! That was epic, Ray! Your hair went all black and white and EVERYTHING. We thought you'd met your rainbow's end!' cried Droplett.

'But . . . the Eye of the Storm . . .' Ray croaked. 'I don't know if I broke the spell?'

'You *did* break it. And we thought it had broken you, but thanks to La Blaze, you're here, and you're OK,' said Snowden. Nim nibbled at Ray's hair, which was (mostly) multicoloured again, apart from a few black and white stripes.

Ray looked up at La Blaze. 'How?'

'Turns out there WAS another way,' said La Blaze, tapping *The Book of Forbidden Forces* with a smile.

'But I thought –' Ray began. But La Blaze held up a hand.

'It's done. Don't worry about anything else. The main thing is, you did it, kid! You closed the Eye of the Storm and broke the spell. But most importantly, you're HERE with us again.'

She ruffled Ray's hair. But Ray couldn't help noticing a sadness in the Sun Weatherling's eyes. And La Blaze's hair was white instead of the usual bright lemon; limp instead of wavy. Her eyes shone grey instead of crystal.

'Are you OK?' asked Ray, feeling worried.

La Blaze waved a hand. 'Ah, I'm fine,' she said, but her voice sounded strained. She chortled lightly, then coughed. 'Just a bit tired after all that snorbing.'

'Thank you for being there for me, La Blaze,' said Ray. 'For saving me from the Shadow Essence at the mill, and risking prison to help us.'

'You know, I'd do anything for you,' said La Blaze, her voice small. 'That's what friends do. You're a special kid, Ray. You helped me when I needed it. I'll never forget that.'

Ray hugged La Blaze tight. But she suddenly felt her heart start beating hard. 'WAIT. Where's Tornadia?' she said, getting up too quickly and making herself go dizzy.

'Hopefully still floating around in that puddle portal you put her in,' said Droplett.

Ray bit her lip. 'I doubt she'll stay in there for long. I mean, she's Tornadia Twist. She survived being inside a snowman for a thousand years . . .'

'Yeah, she's like a bad smell you can't get rid of . . .' said Snowden, raising an eyebrow. Then he winked. Ray gave a small chuckle.

'We can't be sure where she is,' La Blaze said warningly. 'But Tornadia can twist any weather into whatever she pleases. She'll find a way out, no doubt. We have to assume she's still out there somewhere. But the good news is, she'll be incredibly weak. When a Forbidden Spell gets

broken, it severely weakens your power. She'll
be out of action for a bit, at least. That'll give
the Weatherlands enough time to prepare, if she
returns.'

'Speaking of the Weatherlands, we need to go
and save it,' sang Droplett. 'We've got a whole
bunch of cloud-creatures to take home.'

Ray pulled Nim into the biggest hug EVER.
She was so happy to have him back. 'I missed you
SO much!' she said as the cloud-cat nuzzled into
her belly.

She got to her feet slowly. Every limb was
aching and her head felt like it had exploded and
been put back together again. She looked at the
cave wall. The Eye had disappeared.

'Let's go home,' she said to the fluffy clouds
staring at her.

Snowden and Droplett guided the cloud-
creatures out into the sunlight of the beach.

'Hey, La Blaze, which cloud-creature do you
want to ride back to the Weatherlands with us?'
Ray asked. 'I think you'd look brilliant on the

cloud-platypus.'

La Blaze chuckled. 'I think I might stay here for a bit. The sea air is nice.'

'You saved the Weatherlands with me,' Ray said. 'The Council of Forecasters can't possibly send you to prison after this. Come back with us!'

La Blaze lowered herself carefully on to the rocks. 'Kid, this is *your* time. Go show the Weatherlands the amazing Rainbow Weatherling you are,' she said. 'You'd best hurry, though. The cloud-creatures will fade if they're not back with their owners soon.'

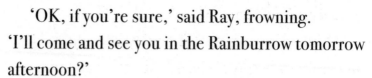

'OK, if you're sure,' said Ray, frowning. 'I'll come and see you in the Rainburrow tomorrow afternoon?'

La Blaze was fiddling with the petals on her sunflower wristbands. 'Yeah . . . I'll see you soon. But you've got to make sure the Weatherlands don't fall apart first. Skedaddle, kid!'

She waved a hand to usher Ray away affectionately. Ray hesitated, then gave La Blaze another big hug before running to her friends who were waiting outside the cave.

It was no longer raining. The air felt calm, and hundreds of cloud-creatures bobbed up and down in the air, eager to return to their Weatherlings.

'I'm riding this one!' said Droplett, swinging herself on to Valianté, the cloud-unicorn who belonged to head of the Council of Forecasters.

Snowden stood next to Waldo the cloud-whale, who was smiling for the first time ever. 'I've always fancied a cloud-whale ride,' Snowden said with a huge grin.

Nim expanded and miaowed, ready for flight.

Ray scrubbed him behind the ears.

'Nim, do you think you can fly like you've never flown before?' she asked. 'We need to guide all the cloud-creatures back home as fast as we can.'

Nim purred and revved up in response.

A fluster of teeny-tiny clouds of no particular shape suddenly came squeaking around Ray's ankles.

'Oh! It's all the baby clouds from the puff pods!' gasped Ray. 'They won't be able to fly yet.'

She bent down and picked up one of the mini clouds. Its tiny eyes looked up at her.

'We'll get you back to the pods where you belong, don't worry,' said Ray, gently tucking as many of the baby clouds into her waistcoat as possible.

Ray mounted Nim's floofy back and turned to the hundreds of cloud-creatures floating on the sandy beach. Then she looked at Snowden and Droplett on the backs of Waldo and Valianté and her heart swelled.

'You've got this, Ray,' said Snowden with a wink.

'Take us home!' yelled Droplett.

'OK, everyone. Follow me!' Ray called out. She leaned forward, ready for flight. 'Up, up and AWAAAAAY!'

The friends took off at super speed. All around them, the sky was full of beautiful, smiling cloud-creatures, all looking forward to being reunited with their Weatherlings.

The friends flew higher and higher until the Earth was no longer visible below them.

'We're almost there!' yelled Ray.

The sky shifted and the Weatherlands shimmered into view.

The whole place seemed to be in hundreds of pieces now. Weather Warriors and Forecasters and other Weatherlings were using their magic to keep as many buildings and houses intact as possible, with magical ice platforms or windy trails or big rain bubbles. The Weatherlands might have been falling apart, but everyone was working TOGETHER.

Ray felt a rush of pride.

But then her chest tightened. A HUGE crack was spreading right into the heart of the city. She felt sure it would break Celestia in two!

'Ray!' cried Droplett from Valianté's back. 'The cloud-creatures are fading!'

The cloud-creatures were fizzling in and out of view like a glitchy film.

'Faster!' Ray shouted. 'Everyone fly faster!'

Nim was already flying as fast as he could. Just a little further! They were SO close now. The cloud-creatures were barely visible. NO! thought Ray. This couldn't be happening!

Ray landed Nim next to the puff pod patch. Snowden and Droplett went tumbling across the mossy ground behind her. The huge crack was appearing ahead of them. Ray clambered to her feet as Waldo and Valianté took off in search of their Weatherlings.

All the cloud-creatures were soaring above

269

the crumbling forest now, spreading out across the Weatherlands, heading for home. The tiny cloud babies erupted from Ray's waistcoat, squeaking and gurgling with joy as they rolled through the air and back into their puff pods, where they would stay until they were picked.

Everything seemed to go very quiet.

'Did it work?' asked Droplett.

The land stopped shaking. The crack in the

ground ahead of them was beginning to fill up with sparkly clouds.

'The cloud magic is returning!' gasped Snowden. 'The cloud-creatures must have got back to their Weatherlings in time!'

Ray could hardly believe it. Snowden and Droplett ran to their friend and hugged her tight.

'You did it, Ray!' cried Droplett.

'WE did it,' Ray corrected with a wink.

CHAPTER 26

STAR OF THE SHOW

A moment later Valianté galloped to a stop before them. Riding on her back was the most important Weatherling in the sky: Flurryweather Floatacious, head of the Council of Forecasters.

The tall Cloud Weatherling with piercing white eyes dismounted and bowed her head. A group of Weather Warrior guards appeared behind her, along with other members of the Council. All of them were smiling.

'Rainbow Grey,' said Flurryweather Floatacious. Her voice was like twinkling wind chimes. 'We owe you our lives.'

'And you owe ME an apology,' said another, much less twinkly voice. Coo La La flew in through the treetops and landed rather ungracefully at the Forecaster's feet with his wings on his hips.

'I do,' acknowledged Flurryweather. 'We are sorry, Mr La La. We should have believed you when you claimed Tornadia Twist was back.'

'Yes, you should,' Coo La La snapped. 'Having said that, compliments to the prison chef. That lasagne was DIVINE.' He strutted over to Ray. 'Where is La Blaze? I think I miss her.'

Ray chuckled. 'La Blaze will be back tomorrow. I think she was a bit tired after helping me fight Tornadia.' She patted the pigeon's head. 'It's good to have you back, Coo La La.'

'Well, of course it is,' the pigeon replied, ruffling his feathers. 'I'm Coo La La, after all.'

'RAY!' shouted another voice from above.

Ray's parents were sitting on Waldo the cloud-whale, who glided down to the forest floor. Cloudia and Haze ran over to their daughter.

'I don't even WANT to know what you've been up to, young lady!' said Cloudia, kissing Ray over and over on the cheeks.

'You broke Waldo,' said Ray's dad.

Ray's heart sank. 'What?' she squeaked.

'You made the old blob SMILE,' Haze replied, patting Waldo's head. 'We are all so proud of you, Ray,' he added quietly.

Ray bit her lip. 'I don't think I ever got round to telling you that I MAY have got expelled from school . . .'

'Well, actually, that's no longer the case,' said a voice that made Ray squirm.

Miss Myst appeared next to Forecaster Flurryweather. 'Today's events have proved that you are a worthy and respected student of Sky Academy and we all owe you our sincere thanks. And perhaps I owe you an apology, but I'm still working on that.'

Then the weirdest thing happened. Miss Myst *smiled*. Snowden gasped and coughed up a snowball.

'Ray Grey,' said Forecaster Flurryweather. 'You put yourself at risk for the well-being of the

Weatherlands. You displayed bravery,
and you helped to defeat a truly terrible Rogue.
You, Snowden Everfreeze, Droplett Dewbells –
the three of you will be given the Weatherlands
Bravery Badge of Honour.'

'That's our girl!' cried Cloudia, fist-pumping
the air.

Ray felt pride fizzing through her. 'Thank you
so much,' she said. 'Although Tornadia's not
really *defeated*. I'm sure she will be back . . .'

Forecaster Flurryweather nodded. 'She will.
But we'll be ready.'

More Cloud Weatherlings arrived on their cloud-creatures, cheering with delight. Among the growing crowd was Aunt Foggaleena. Ray's heart sank as the pointy-faced woman marched over with little Cloudiculus in her arms. She waited for her aunt to blame her for something.

Instead, Foggaleena offered a hand. Ray stared for a moment before taking it slowly. Foggaleena shook Ray's hand once. There was something different about her aunt's eyes. Was that a hint of warmth . . .?

'I think this is Foggaleena's way of saying sorry,' whispered Haze in Ray's ear. 'Just go with it.'

As Ray watched Cloudiculus flail in his mother's arms, she suddenly had a brilliant idea.

'Hey, Aunty?' she said. 'Since we're all here, how about we try again with the puff pod picking? Cloudiculus is still owed a cloud-companion.'

Foggaleena's eyes brightened, and Ray got something a smidge closer to a smile. 'My darling Cloudiculus DOES deserve it,' her aunt replied, placing the baby down into the puff pod patch.

Cloudiculus rolled over and farted before prodding at a pod.

'A puff pod has been chosen!' sang Aunt Foggaleena.

Nim purred merrily and wrapped himself around Ray's shoulders as Ray picked the puff pod stem and held it out to her toddler cousin. Cloudiculus stared as the petals began to unfurl. Foggaleena shifted impatiently. The crowd watched with bated breath.

Inside the puff pod was the teeniest, tiniest cloud.

'I've never seen anything so small,' said Droplett, squinting.

Snowden adjusted his glasses. 'I think it's a cloud-flea.'

'A cloud-FLEA?' cried Foggaleena. 'But every one of my children have had cloud-birds!'

'Being different isn't such a bad thing,' said Ray, twirling a strand of yellow hair. 'Even the smallest creature can be the mightiest.'

The Von Fluff cloud-birds gathered and
welcomed the cloud-flea under their wings,
swirling around and creating a beautiful cloudy
formation. Nim joined in with the floofy display,
followed by Waldo and the other cloud-creatures.

Ray sat on a tree stump with Snowden and
Droplett and told them all about her short time
in the Aurora Borealis.

'I can't believe you were IN the Aurora!' said
Droplett. 'You were like, DEAD.'

Ray giggled. 'It was nice to meet Rainbow
Beard,' she said.

'What do you think Rainbow Beard's gift

IS?' asked Snowden.

'I've no idea,' said Ray. 'But I'm a bit disappointed I won't have the ability to make beards now. I think I'd have suited a beard.'

The friends all giggled.

'Maybe this secret powerful gift will help us finally stop Tornadia once and for all?' said Droplett.

'I hope so,' said Ray.

Forecaster Flurryweather tapped Ray on the shoulder. 'Ray, we know that La Blaze left the Rainburrow.'

Ray grimaced. 'Please don't send her to prison,' she urged the head of the Council. 'She helped us save the Weatherlands. I couldn't have done any of this without her.'

'Oh, I know that,' said Flurryweather. 'She is hereby released from burrow arrest and will be receiving a Bravery Badge of Honour too. I thought you'd like to tell her.'

Ray flew as fast as she could down to the Earth beach to tell La Blaze the good news. It was night-time, but the moonlight shone brightly on the sand.

'La Blaze!' Ray called.

But her friend was nowhere to be seen.

Ray walked into the cave. 'La Blaaaaze?!' she called out, her voice echoing all around. 'I have EXCELLENT news! I couldn't wait to tell you. La Blaze? Where are you?'

As Ray made her way deeper into the cave, she almost tripped over something. *The Book of Forbidden Forces* lay open on one of the rocks, barely visible in the darkness.

'Oops! I can't believe I left this behind,' gasped Ray. 'I need to return this to Gusty Gavin so he can hide it away again.'

But then Ray noticed something else. Two faintly glowing sunflowers lay on the open pages. La Blaze's sunflower wristbands . . . the very things she used to channel her magic.

Ray saw that the pages of the book were open

on a spell. But it wasn't the Eye of the Storm.

'*Resurrection Spell*,' Ray read aloud.
She focused on the words, carefully using the
faint glow of the sunflowers as a torch.

You must be sure before performing this spell.
Sing these words to the Weatherling you wish
to give your life to.

Return again, you'll be OK,
What's mine is yours. You're here to stay.

Ray stared at the page. It was the song she had
heard when she was in the Aurora.

Nim purred sadly. Ray picked up the two
sunflowers. Her throat tightened.

'La Blaze . . .' she whispered. 'She used a
Forbidden Spell to save my life, Nim. She gave up
her life, for mine.'

Ray bowed her head and held the sunflower
wrist bands to her chest.

As her tears fell, she spotted someone standing

on the beach, just visible under the waning Moon.

'La Blaze?' said Ray, wiping her eyes.

'LA BLAZE!' She ran as fast as she could towards the figure. 'I thought you were . . .'

But something wasn't right. La Blaze was all shimmery and transparent, just like the ancient Rainbow Weatherlings in the Aurora.

'La Blaze?' said Ray.

'Don't be sad, kid,' said La Blaze gently. She was already fading away.

'This can't be the end,' said Ray desperately. 'There MUST be something else to help.'

La Blaze placed a sparkling hand gently on Ray's shoulder and shook her head.

'But it's not time,' Ray sniffed. Nim attempted to nuzzle the ghostly Weatherling.

'I did my time,' said La Blaze with a smile.

Ray let out a sob. 'I can't do this without you.'

La Blaze chuckled lightly. 'Sure you can, kid! All I did was keep those rainbow notes organised and make a big hole in the Rainburrow wall. Now there'll always be something to remind you of me.'

Ray couldn't help smiling through her tears.

'I'm going to miss you so much,' she said.

'I'll never really be gone,' said La Blaze, looking up at the night sky. 'You see all those stars? They're tiny suns. Tiny glimmers of the past. Great Sun Weatherlings, continuing to shine.' She was a golden ghost, barely visible now. 'The people we love never really leave us.

Besides, I've always wanted to be the STAR of the show!'

She slowly rose into the air in a shimmering golden mist. It was beautiful.

'I'm proud of you, kid,' said La Blaze's voice, a faint whisper in the air. 'Always be you.' And La Blaze DeLight's golden glimmer whirled up into the night sky.

It took a few weeks for the Weatherlands to get back to normal.

Every Weatherling helped and worked together to repair what had been damaged. Ray's family home at Cloud Nine was back in the sky

with the other pod houses in the Cloudimulus Suburbs, and the City of Celestia was glimmering once again in the Sunflower's light. Sky Academy was closed for repairs as whole branches had snapped and the Thermomoteering temperature pyramids had been lost through a crack in the ground. Ray wasn't TOO sad about that.

Once the school opened again, Ray returned *The Book of Forbidden Forces* to a very relieved Gusty Gavin, and the Council of Forecasters started preparing for the return of Tornadia Twist, deploying more Weather Warriors than ever before to patrol the Earth and skies.

Ray stood in the Sunflower field and stared up at the large statue of La Blaze that had been built in the Sun Weatherling's honour. She had become a part of history, for her bravery and kindness. For never giving up on Ray.

'La Blaze really was a hero,' said Droplett, beside Ray.

'I knew that from the very first moment I read about her adventures,' said Ray softly.

She looked to the horizon. A small part of her would always be hoping that La Blaze might come rolling through the flowers on her glowing sun skates. What she didn't expect was to see a pigeon strutting towards her.

'ACHOO!' Snowden sneezed. 'Coo La La?'

Coo La La tipped his tiny top hat. 'Whose sidekick am I meant to be now?' he said, peering up at the statue. A small tear rolled down his feathered face. 'Eurgh. Hayfever!' he said, wiping the tear quickly and composing himself.

'I didn't think you liked being called La Blaze's sidekick?' said Ray.

'Sometimes you don't realise what you have until it's gone,' Coo La La said. Then he cleared his throat. 'I guess I'll be *your* sidekick now.'

Ray burst out laughing. Then she offered a hand. Coo La La shook it with a wing.

'Welcome to the gang!' Ray said.

Snowden sighed. 'I best find some allergy medicine if you're going to be here all the time,' he said.

'I could replace *you*?' suggested Coo La La.
'Great idea!' said Droplett, nudging Snowden
in the ribs affectionately.

'You're all awful,' said Snowden with a big smile on his face.

The friends spent a little longer with the La Blaze statue, the light from the Great Sunflower glimmering on La Blaze's beautiful face.

'I still can't believe she's gone,' said Coo La La.

'She's not really gone,' said Ray finally. 'Come on, I'll show you.'

The friends and Coo La La took to the skies on the back of Nim. Ray looked across the City of Celestia. The Sky Academy weathervane glimmered in the Sunflower's light, representing the different types of weather magic. Except now, at the very top of the vane, a set of multicoloured rainbow ribbons gently billowed in the breeze. All the weather, together as one.

They kept on flying until the light of the Weatherlands faded and the friends entered the night side of Earth, which was shimmering with millions of stars. One star was twinkling brighter than all the rest.

'There she is,' Ray said with a smile. 'Star of the show!'

Ray held up her staff and let the biggest, brightest rainbow stretch across the night sky. 'This one's for you, La Blaze,' she cried.

Ray, Snowden and Droplett soared through the colours and twinkles, their arms linked and their hearts full of love and hope. Coo La La flew alongside, and Nim's long pink trail followed close behind.

Even though Tornadia was still out there somewhere, Ray felt hopeful. She knew that with the help of her friends and family they could beat her. Together, they could achieve ANYTHING.

THE END

DISCOVER A WORLD OF MAGIC
BEHIND EVERY RAINBOW!

Join Ray and her friends
for a brand-new
WHIRLWIND adventure!

Tornadia Twist is BACK ...
and this time she won't stop
until she has destroyed the
Weatherlands forever.

Do Ray and her friends have
what it takes to save the world
from eternal darkness?

Find out in
the next thrilling

book – coming soon!